ELLA OF ALL-OF-A-KIND FAMILY

ELLA
OF
ALL-OF-A-KIND FAMILY

Sydney Taylor

A YEARLING BOOK

Published by
Dell Publishing
a division of
Bantam Doubleday Dell Publishing Group, Inc.
666 Fifth Avenue
New York, New York 10103

ISBN: 0-440-42252-3

Printed in the United States of America

One Previous Edition

May 1989

10 9 8 7 6 5 4 3

CWO

to Ella—so gifted, yet ever aware
of the potential in others, inspiring
them to achieve their goals

Contents

1

No Place Like Home

"Jules!" Ella whispered the endearing name.

Those happy days before he went off to war . . . strolling along, hand in hand, talking and laughing together, disposing of the future as if it were ours alone. It was as if Jules was a part of my childhood—as if we had always known each other. . . .

Ella sighed. Will it still be the same between us? After all, we've been apart from each other for more than a year. People change—even in normal times. With all that a soldier goes through, far away from home and loved ones, will he—can he—be the same dear Jules I have always known?

And what will he think of me, after all those chic French girls? She studied herself in the mirror, patting the neat coil of hair at the nape of her neck.

Not quite as attractive as my sister Henny's golden curls. But still it has a lovely sheen, and the color, blue-black almost, does set off my white skin nicely. Jules always liked my hair. . . .

Now for the final touch. Quickly, before anyone caught her in the act, she sprinkled some talcum powder into the palm of her hand and dabbed it carefully over her nose and chin. "There! That's much better," she reassured the face in the mirror.

What would Mama say if I started using real face powder? Most of the girls in the office do. They say it really stays on. Not like this baby stuff. And it's perfumed. Next payday I'll get myself a box.

After all, I'm eighteen. What's wrong with a girl my age trying to improve her looks? It's 1919. Times have changed. Some girls even use rouge. Of course I wouldn't go that far.

One last pat at her hair—a tug at her dress, and Ella felt she was ready. She'd wait for Jules in the parlor.

Alas, the parlor was already taken over by her four sisters and her brother.

"Do you all have to sit in here?" she inquired icily. "What's the matter with the rest of the house all of a sudden?"

"We want to see Jules, too," littlest sister Gertie piped up.

Precisely at that moment the downstairs buzzer sounded.

"Oh dear!" Ella exclaimed. "Mama, please tick back!" she yelled into the kitchen and began frantically shooing the others from the room.

"All right, we're going. Don't get so upset," Henny said. "Anyone would think we were going to take a bite out of her precious boyfriend."

Thank goodness, she was alone! Quickly she released the catch on the parlor door which opened onto the hall. She wavered a moment, torn between the urge to rush to greet Jules on the landing or to have him discover her in a charming setting. The setting won.

She sat down at the piano, spreading her skirt so that it

fell in a graceful swirl over the piano stool. Her fingers touched the keys. The next moment they were playing in soft accompaniment as she sang:

> *Just a little love, a little kiss*
> *I would give you all my life for this....*

Excitement made her voice tremble, for even as the song flowed through the room, she could feel his presence coming toward her.

She turned. There he was, framed motionless in the doorway.

The song faded into silence. Jules moved forward.

"Ella, that was so beautiful."

She'd forgotten how deep his voice was. She gazed up at him. Because his face was tanned, his eyes seemed bluer than she'd remembered. She smiled. Oh how wonderful—how utterly wonderful it was to see him! Their eyes met, his arms reached out to her—

The portieres rustled.

"Oh—excuse me!" Papa's voice shattered the rapturous moment.

Quickly Ella averted her gaze as Jules's arms dropped stiffly to his sides.

Papa paused in the middle of the room, a crumpled newspaper in his hand, his glasses perched at the end of his nose. Ella realized he had wandered in seeking some peace and quiet, forgetting entirely about Jules's coming.

"Oh," Papa scratched his head uncertainly. "Who's that? It's Jules—Jules! My, you look so different. For a moment, I couldn't believe it." He caught hold of Jules's hand and began pumping it vigorously. "Welcome! Welcome home.

3

Thank God you're home safe. We were all so worried about you."

He settled himself on the couch. "I myself never had to fight in a war. But I can well imagine how terrible it was for our boys over there. And now," he poked his finger at the newspaper headline, "I don't know. The way things are in such a muddle. It was supposed to be the war to end all wars. Instead, every country is trying to take advantage for itself. Look, even in our own country, the way those senators are fighting President Wilson. Let me ask you, do you really think a League of Nations can amount to something?"

Oh no! Ella despaired. It looks like Papa's getting ready for a long discussion. Doesn't he realize we want to be alone?

Just then Mama emerged through the portieres with little Charlie tagging after.

Ella perked up. Mama will understand.

"Papa," Mama said at once, "you know that shelf in the kitchen where the clock stands? It's coming loose. You'd better fix it right away."

"Right this minute?"

"Yes. Right away. This minute!" Mama replied, fixing him with a meaningful stare.

Papa remained seated with a puzzled expression on his face. He glanced first at Jules and then at Ella. "Oh," he said suddenly, "that's right. I'll attend to it right away."

He stood up, folded his newspaper hurriedly and shuffled out of the room.

"Well now." Mama turned to Jules with a tone of having solved a problem. "Nice to see you, Jules. You look wonderful. Come, take off your coat and sit down. Make

4

yourself comfortable. Ella, what kind of a hostess are you, letting Jules stand around with his coat on?"

Oh dear, Ella thought, now it's Mama hovering over Jules like a mother hen.

"It's getting pretty cold out, isn't it?" Mama rattled on.

Jules removed his coat and remained standing, holding it awkwardly in his arms.

"Jules, you're in civvies!" Ella exclaimed.

"Civvies?" Mama repeated.

"No more uniform," Jules explained. He straightened up self-consciously as Mama looked him up and down.

"You look very nice in your blue suit," Mama said with a little laugh. "You know what Aunt Lena always says, 'If a man doesn't look good in a blue suit, he'll never look good in anything.' "

Jules grinned sheepishly, shifting his coat from one arm to the other.

"Ella, why don't you take his coat?" Mama ordered. "Do sit down, Jules."

Jules obliged. Leaning back, he crossed his legs in an effort to be casual. Ella could sense his discomfort, but Mama kept chatting away cheerily.

From somewhere Mama's inevitable knitting appeared. On the instant, the needles began clicking away beneath her nimble fingers.

Ye gods! Ella fretted. How much longer does Mama intend to stay? Her eyes met Jules's and telegraphed, "I know. But what can I do?"

"And your mother? How is she?" Mama went on. "I can just imagine how happy she must be to have you back home, safe and sound."

During all this time, a strangely quiet Charlie stood by.

5

Now suddenly, he ran up to Jules and pulled at his arm. "Where's your uniform?" he asked,

Jules tousled the boy's blond hair. "All packed away, Charlie."

Charlie continued to stare up at him. "Aren't you a soldier anymore?"

"Nope. The war's over, Charlie."

"Thank God!" Mama added.

Conversation seemed to have run out. Jules swung a leg back and forth, back and forth. The knitting needles clicked loudly in the void.

All at once Jules sat up. "I almost forgot. I've got something for you, Charlie."

"For me?"

Jules dangled a small paper bag in the air.

Charlie snatched it and ripped it open. "Ooh! An Indian Bar!" he squealed. Greedily he bit into the peanuts and chocolate.

"Charlie!" scolded Mama. "Where are your manners?"

Mouth full, Charlie mumbled, "Thanks," then added reluctantly, "anybody wanna bite?"

It seemed no one did, so Charlie munched away blissfully.

It was nice of Jules to remember my little brother, Ella thought. You can tell he likes children. I'm glad. I couldn't possibly care for a man who didn't.

Jules was smiling at her. He inclined his head slightly, indicating Mama, his eyebrows raised questioningly.

Ella went over to Mama and whispered, "Mama, please!"

Mama rose quickly. "Charlie," she announced, "it's time for you to go to bed."

6

"Aw, everybody's always telling me it's time to go to bed," grumbled Charlie. "Do I have to?"

"Yes you have to," Mama insisted, and marshaled him out.

Alone at last! Jules relaxed against the couch. Ella nestled beside him. He reached for her hand and their fingers intertwined.

Jules's voice broke into the stillness. "I'm lucky. I got a job today."

"A job? You're not going back to school?"

"I can't now. It's the middle of the term. Besides, I'm not going back—not in the daytime that is. I'm twenty years old! It's time I began working. Since my father died, my mother has had to work doubly hard to raise the family. Of course my oldest sister is married, but remember there are two younger sisters still at home. I can't go on expecting my mother to support me. So . . ."

Brr-rrr-ring! The peal of the telephone tore through his words. Brr-rrr-ring! The parlor door flew open and Henny burst in.

"I think it's for me."

"So did you have to come through here to answer it?" demanded Ella.

Henny grinned. "Hi, Jules!" She tossed her head saucily and disappeared through the portieres.

Ella threw up her hands. "That Henny! The phone's in the dining room. There was absolutely no need for her to come barging in here. Well, never mind. You were telling me about a job."

"It's with an import and export firm."

"Oh."

There was no time for further explanations, for the

sound of approaching steps could plainly be heard. Again the portieres parted and in sidled Charlotte and Gertie.

"Hello, Jules," Charlotte and Gertie chorused.

Their gaze slid sidewise to each other, lips twitching with the effort to suppress the giggles. They tried covering their mouths but it was no use. They exploded in a cascade of titters.

After a few more sputterings, Charlotte raised her hand and waved a small fluttering good-bye. Gertie followed suit and both backed up through the portieres.

Jules chuckled. "They're cute."

"Couple of sillies," Ella said. "They're at that age, I guess. Tell me, what sort of work will you be doing?"

"Bookkeeping."

"Will you like that?"

"It's a job, and they seem like nice people. Anyway, it's not going to be forever. I've thought a lot about the future. The future's terribly important to me—to us."

He put a hand under her chin, lifted her face and kissed her. And Ella knew then that no matter how long their separation, Jules had not changed. He loved her!

"Er—hello," a voice spoke up timidly.

They sprang apart. Middle sister Sarah had slipped in so quietly, they had not heard her. There she stood with a book clutched tightly to her chest.

"Oh! Excuse me, please!" she implored. "You look so different without your uniform, Jules." She flushed with confusion. "Oh, I didn't mean that you don't look good. It's just that, it's different, that's all," she finished lamely.

"It's okay. Don't worry about it," Jules assured her. "What's that book you're hugging?"

"My algebra. I'm in the middle of my homework. There's

8

one problem I'm really stuck with. I asked Henny but she says she's forgotten everything she ever learned about algebra. Do you think maybe—you could help me with it?"

Jules's shoulders lifted resignedly. "All right. Let's have a look."

What a time to pick for an algebra lesson, Ella fumed. She and Sarah had always been very close despite the difference of four years in their ages. But right now she was really annoyed with her. Her patience was at an end.

She stalked out of the parlor, past Mama's and Papa's bedroom, through the small alcove where Charlie, already in bed, popped up curiously as she sped by, into Charlotte's and Gertie's room, then Henny's quarters, and finally into the dining room where the family was assembled.

Arms akimbo, her small frame bristling with anger, she lashed out, "How in heaven's name can a person get any privacy in this house? Honestly, sometimes I wish I were an only child. At least then I'd have a chance. Jules came to see me—*me*! Not you! We haven't been able to exchange two words without some member of the family butting in!"

"All right, Ella, don't get so excited," Mama soothed. "Charlie!" she yelled suddenly. "What are you doing in here? Back to your bed! And be quick about it! Do you hear?"

Mama turned back to Ella. "Compose yourself. Now that everyone has got a look at your boyfriend, they won't bother you anymore."

But Ella was still riled up. "It's rotten being the oldest!" She thrust a finger sharply at Charlotte and Gertie. "By the time these two start going out with boys, they'll have it easy. Nobody'll even be interested."

"Who's interested?" Henny interrupted. "We were just being polite."

"Thanks! So you were all polite. Now please—everybody—stay out! For the next half hour at least!"

She spun around and flounced out.

Back in the parlor, she heard Sarah say, "Thanks so much, Jules. You'd make an awfully good teacher." Flitting past Ella, she flashed her a bright smile. "He explains things so well."

"I see she's got your future mapped out for you," Ella remarked.

Jules grinned. He drew Ella to the couch and put his arm around her.

"No, Ella. No teaching for me. I used to dream about being a doctor, but that would take too long and too much money. Still, I want to be some kind of professional rather than just a businessman. My uncle, the optometrist, says it's an interesting career with a future, and he would help me. I could go to school at night. What do you think, Ella?"

"It sounds like a . . ."

Were the portieres moving? Or was it just her imagination? Was someone hiding behind them? Who would dare? There was someone! Two little pink feet were plainly visible below.

Sliding out of Jules's arm, Ella crept stealthily toward the feet. She yanked the portieres apart. A startled Charlie, in his nightshirt, stood blinking up at her!

"Charlie, is this a way to behave?" Ella scolded.

Chuckling, Jules put his hand into his pocket. "Don't

10

you dare, Jules!" Ella cried. "Don't you dare give him anything! I'm going right in to tell Mama!"

"Oh, don't be too hard on him, Ella," Jules replied, putting a nickel into Charlie's hand. "It's a time-honored custom, you know."

"Ooh, thanks!" Charlie whooped joyfully. "I'm going right into my bed, I promise." As he scooted off, he turned and whispered back. "And don't tell Mama."

Jules looked at Ella. "Well, who's next? I feel as if I were courting the whole family. Now, before anyone else comes in—" His strong arms lifted her off the floor as he planted a resounding kiss on her cheek. Swinging her around the room, he sang into her ear: "There's no place like home sweet home, there's no place like home."

By the time he set her down, they were both helpless with laughter. "Come on," Jules cried, "let's get out of here. We'll walk and talk. I want to hear about everything that went on this past year. You'll tell me about your singing lessons, and your job—everything! And when we get too cold, we can drop into Ziggy's Ice-cream Parlor for some hot chocolate and cookies."

2

A Bang-up Time

"Charlotte," Mama said, "Aunt Fanny would like you to mind Ruthie tonight. She and Uncle Joe have to go somewhere."

Lost in the enchanted world of a storybook, Charlotte heard nothing.

Mama raised her voice. "Charlotte! I'm talking to you!"

Charlotte's blue eyes fluttered upward. "Huh?"

"Aunt Fanny wants you to mind Ruthie tonight."

Charlotte came to life. "Ooh yes!"

"You're lucky," Sarah commented. "Aunt Fanny always asks you."

"It's really Ruthie who wants her," Mama explained. "She says Charlotte thinks up such interesting things to do and tells such good stories."

"I wouldn't mind earning the money myself once in a while," Sarah said.

"What for?" scoffed Henny. "You'd only put the dime in your savings account. Now if it were me . . ."

"If it were you," interrupted Mama, "the dime would be spent even before you earned it."

"Want to come along?" Charlotte asked Gertie.

Gertie hesitated.

"Aunt Fanny's very generous," Charlotte urged. "She

12

always leaves such good things around for me, like candy and cookies. I'll give you half the money."

Gertie brightened. "Okay."

So that evening, the two sisters walked arm in arm to Aunt Fanny's house.

"Oh, the two of you! How nice!" Aunt Fanny cried as she opened the door. "Ruthie, look who's here," she called out to her daughter, who came running. "Your two cousins. They're going to stay with you while Daddy and I go out. Isn't that nice?"

Little Ruthie hopped up and down gleefully. "Gertie, you going to play with Charlotte and me?"

"Uh-huh."

After instructing Charlotte what to do and when, Aunt Fanny donned her hat and coat. "Good night, Ruthie darling," she said, embracing her. "Be a good girl and listen to what Charlotte and Gertie tell you and maybe Mommy and Daddy will bring you back something special."

"What'll you bring?"

"You'll see. Good night, girls." And Aunt Fanny shepherded her husband out the door.

"Have a good time," the children yelled after them.

No sooner had the door closed, when Ruthie asked, "What'll we do first, Charlotte?"

Charlotte's brow wrinkled. "Well now, let's see. . . . I know! We'll make paper patterns."

"What's that?"

"Come on. We'll get the scissors and some paper napkins and I'll show you."

Soon all three were seated around the kitchen table. Charlotte picked up a napkin, folded it in half, and then again in quarters. "Now watch," she said.

13

Carefully spiraling the folded paper, she snipped this way and that. The cut-off pieces fell away, the paper unfolded, and there, spread out before Ruthie's astonished eyes, was a lovely lace doily.

"It's beautiful!" Ruthie exclaimed. "Now you make one, Gertie."

Gertie cut away cautiously and turned out a pretty pattern of her own.

"Now lemme try," Ruthie said.

"All right, but you'll have to be careful with the scissors," warned Charlotte.

"Oh I will! I'll be very careful," Ruthie promised.

Charlotte tried to guide her little hand, but Ruthie would have none of it. "No!" she yelled, shaking her head vehemently. "I wanna do it all by myself."

She worked away stubbornly, her lower lip sucked in, her straight brown hair straggling across her face. Repeatedly she pushed the locks back only to have them tumble forward again.

"How can she see anything with that hair in her eyes all the time?" Gertie cried. "Couldn't we pin it back?"

"It wouldn't stay. Her hair's too soft. Say!" Charlotte's face lit up with sudden inspiration. "Why don't we cut bangs for her?"

Gertie looked dubious. "Gee, do you think we ought to? Aunt Fanny might not like it."

"Nonsense," pooh-poohed Charlotte. "She'd love it! Why with Ruthie's little round face, she'd look cute as a bug with bangs. Ruthie, wouldn't you rather have pretty bangs on your forehead instead of that long messy hair?"

"You mean like Buster Brown in the funnies?"

"Uh-huh. It'll be so much more comfortable. Prettier too."

"Ooh yes," Ruthie agreed, charmed by the idea of a new hairdo.

Gertie still had her doubts. "But will you be able to do it all right, Charlotte?"

"There's nothing to it. It's simple." Charlotte exuded supreme confidence. "You just take the scissors and cut across the forehead. Miss Ruth," she bowed ceremoniously, "when you have finished what you're doing, will you kindly step into our barbershop?"

Ruthie was quite ready to abandon the napkins for this new game. "I'm finished already," she chirped.

Charlotte pulled a chair into the center of the room.

"Upsa daisy!" she cried, sweeping Ruthie off her feet and onto the seat.

"Now with your permission, madam." Briskly she flip-flapped a towel and with a grand flourish tied it under Ruthie's chin. Picking up the scissors, she held them aloft, clicking them open and shut.

The click, click sound seemed a bit menacing to Ruthie. Warily her big brown eyes followed Charlotte's every move.

Now Charlotte was bending over her, scissors poised. Ruthie's shoulders hunched. The metal felt cold against her temple. She squeezed her eyes shut so tight her face screwed up like a small monkey's.

Snip—scrunch—snip! Wisps of hair started floating down into Ruthie's lap. Scrunch-snip-scrunch! It wasn't scary anymore. Ruthie relaxed.

"There you are!" Charlotte announced with satisfaction, stepping back to survey the effect.

"Do I look nice?" Ruthie asked.

"Very nice," admitted Gertie. "Only . . . Charlotte, don't

15

you think it ought to be straightened out a bit? The bangs look sort of uneven."

"Hold up your head, Ruthie," directed Charlotte.

"Hmm. You're right, Gertie. It is a little bit shorter on the right. Well, we can fix that easily enough. Just a bit here—a tiny snip there—a little more—just a bit. . . ."

Another look and both sisters agreed that now the bangs were shorter on the left. Charlotte frowned. "I can't understand why it doesn't come out even."

"I think you ought to put something with a straight edge up against her forehead and follow the line," advised Gertie. "Like a ruler. That way you'd be sure to come out straight."

Charlotte's face lit up. "I have a much better idea." She opened the door of the dish closet.

"What are you looking for?"

"This!" Charlotte held up a mixing bowl. "Turn it upside down and presto! You have a beautiful china hat with a perfect edge for cutting bangs."

Ruthie sat very still as Charlotte put the mixing bowl on her head.

"Oh madam," Charlotte gushed, "such a becoming hat! You look just gorgeous—simply gorgeous!"

"Lemme see. I wanna see," Ruthie cried.

Gertie held up a shiny tin cookie jar. Ruthie giggled at her reflection. "I look so funny."

The bowl slipped down over her eyes.

"Oops!" yelled Charlotte, rushing to the rescue. "Hey, where are you?" she asked laughingly as she maneuvered the bowl back into place. It slipped again, this time over one eye, giving Ruthie a rakish look.

"You hang on to it, Gertie," Charlotte commanded, "or

we'll never get this done. Hold the bowl so that only the tip ends of the bangs show. There—that's fine! Close your eyes, Ruthie. I don't want to get any hairs in them."

Ruthie sat stiffly while the scissors clipped away.

"Now, off with the bowl, Gertie. I'm all through."

"Gosh, Charlotte!" Gertie sounded dismayed. "It's so short!"

"The shorter the better," Charlotte said, trying to sound convincing. "What do you want bangs to do? Hang down so far over her eyes, she'll need a Seeing Eye dog? I think they're exactly the right length, and it makes Ruthie look very pretty."

But Ruthie was a bit doubtful. She rubbed a hand over her forehead. "It feels so short."

"How can we tell what she looks like the way she's messing her hair up?" Charlotte said. "Let's comb it out. Then we'll see."

They brushed and combed but some long strands of hair were still visible among shorter ones.

"How'd you happen to miss those, Charlotte?"

"I don't know. Maybe her hair wasn't parted exactly in the middle. I should have straightened it out first before I began cutting. Oh well," Charlotte made light of the whole business, "it doesn't really matter. All I have to do is snip off those few extra hairs and it'll be fine." She picked up the scissors. A snip here, a snip there, a snip everywhere. "There! That does it!"

Gertie gulped. "Gosh, I never saw bangs zigzag all the way up to the ears before. It looks peculiar."

"What's pe-culiar?" Ruthie asked.

"Oh nothing!" snapped Charlotte. She turned on Gertie. "I like it this way. It gives her face a sort of"—she fished about for the right words—"a clean, open look," she ended triumphantly.

Anxious to have it over with, Gertie allowed herself to be persuaded. "Well, maybe, but you ought at least try to even it out. The right side is a good half inch longer than the left."

"Can you fix it, Charlotte?" Ruthie quavered anxiously.

Charlotte sheared away.

Gertie clapped her hands to her head. "Just look at what you're doing! Now the left side's longer!"

The scissors slid over to the left. Snip—snip! By now the towel was overflowing with hair.

"You're only making it worse all the time!" wailed Gertie.

"I am not!" Charlotte retorted, but not too confidently. She chewed on a fingernail. "Say!" she exclaimed, her eyes alight with renewed enthusiasm. "You know what would be really attractive? If I sort of graduate it around, starting very short in the front like this, and gradually leaving the hair longer as you work around toward the back."

"Sounds crazy to me."

"That's because you have no imagination. Once you actually see it, you'll feel different about it. It'll give a lovely sweep to the hair."

"Please, Charlotte," Gertie begged, unconvinced, "don't cut any more."

But there was no staying Charlotte's vision. Already clumps of hair were falling onto the towel as well as on the floor.

By now the barber game was getting too much for Ruthie. "No more," she yelled shaking her cropped head. "I don't want you to cut my hair no more!"

"Please, Ruthie," Charlotte pleaded, "just a teeny bit more and I'll be all finished."

Charlotte kept cutting away as best she could in between Ruthie's wriggling protests and Gertie's alarums. At last she gave up. "Well, that's it," she said, removing the towel. "I can't do any more."

"I should say not," Gertie whispered. "There's more hair on the floor than on her head." She groaned. "Aunt Fanny'll have a fit. And I wouldn't blame her one bit. Who ever saw a haircut like this?"

"Some people have no appreciation for originality," Charlotte countered. "Why must everybody look exactly like everybody else? I think it's so much more interesting this way—different somehow."

"It's different all right," agreed Gertie. "All ziggity-zaggity!"

Ruthie, who had dashed into the bedroom meanwhile for a view of herself in the dresser mirror, came running back. She planted herself before Charlotte, her face all crumpled up. "What did you do? You mur-der-er you!" she screamed, bursting into tears.

Taken aback, Charlotte began biting her nails, not knowing what else to do. After a while, she knelt down and tried to gather the sobbing little girl to her. "Look Ruthie, I'm awfully sorry you don't like it, but honest, it's not bad at all."

Ruthie pulled away and sought the comfort of Gertie's shoulder. Tears streamed down her face. "You're just saying that," she cried. "You know yourself, it's horrible—horrible. Even Gertie thinks so."

Gertie didn't respond. She could only look reproachfully at Charlotte as she patted the weeping Ruthie.

19

"A sweet little girl like you could never look horrible," Charlotte said.

But Ruthie was inconsolable. She wept and wept.

"It'll grow back. It's not going to stay that way forever," Charlotte went on. "So what's the use making such a fuss about it?"

Ruthie only sobbed the harder.

"If I'd had any idea you were going to carry on this way, I never would have bothered in the first place." Charlotte tried to sound miffed. "Believe me, it was no cinch cutting your hair. With all that straggly stuff hanging down your face, you looked like a witch. I did you a big favor cutting it off."

"S-some favor!" sobbed Ruthie.

"It certainly was! Why, snip-snip, and I changed that dreadful witch into a darling little elf!"

Ruthie stopped right in the middle of a great big sob. One eye peeked through her fingers. "A little elf?" she repeated.

"Of course!" Charlotte said as heartily as she could manage. She was beginning to have her own misgivings. "Oh yes," she went on, "that's what you are, Ruthie—a darling little elf. Of course, if later on, you'd rather not be an elf, why then in a few weeks your hair will grow in anyway, and you can change into something else—a fairy maybe. Come on, little elf, let's get ready for bed and I'll tell you a wonderful story about a little elf named Ruthie."

Sniffing back her tears, Ruthie wiped her eyes with the back of her hand. Soon the sobs subsided into small hiccups. "First—tell me—the story," she demanded.

So Charlotte took her on her lap and began a tale of Ruthie, the elf. In a little while, it seemed as if the whole

20

hair-cutting episode was a thing of the past. Ruthie went off to bed without a murmur.

Gertie surveyed the kitchen barbershop. "This floor is one grand mess!"

"We'd better get busy and clean it up right away!" Charlotte exclaimed, dashing for the broom and dustpan.

Hardly had everything been put to rights and the last wisp of hair dumped into the garbage pail when they heard the key being turned in the hall-door lock.

Gertie wrung her hands. "Oh, Charlotte! Here they come. What'll we do?"

"Oh what are you getting so nervous about?" Charlotte cried in a huff. "It's not as bad as you make it out. I'm sure Aunt Fanny will appreciate what we've done. Ruthie's hair will be so easy to manage. No tangles—no snarls—quick washing."

Nonetheless, she lost no time bundling herself up in her hat and coat.

"Hurry up, Gertie! Get your things on. It's pretty late, you know. We gotta get home. We don't want to waste time standing around gabbing."

Gertie needed no urging. They were both ready for instant flight when Aunt Fanny and Uncle Joe came into the kitchen.

"Well, was Ruthie a good girl?" Aunt Fanny greeted. "No trouble?"

"No trouble at all," Charlotte replied. "Well, we'd better go. It's kind of late. Good night, Aunt Fanny, Uncle Joe." Charlotte pushed Gertie toward the door.

"Hey, just a minute!" Uncle Joe shouted after them.

The girls stopped dead in their tracks.

"What—is—it?" Gertie's voice quavered.

21

Uncle Joe smiled. "Don't you want to get paid?"

"Oh—that's right . . . thank you," Charlotte said, taking the dime.

"Want me to walk you home?" Uncle Joe asked.

"You don't have to. It's not that late," Charlotte answered quickly. Pulling open the door, she yanked Gertie out after her.

"Good night!" they yelled back and bolted down the stairs.

At breakfast there was a phone call for Mama. Gertie and Charlotte stopped eating. They sat very still.

In a few minutes, Mama came striding back into the kitchen.

"That was Aunt Fanny on the phone. Was she upset! She was almost crying. Well, Charlotte. Well, Gertie?" Mama looked sternly from one to the other.

The rest of the family stared at the two lowered heads.

"What's this all about?" Ella asked.

"Search me," Henny replied. "Whatever it is, I had absolutely nothing to do with it."

"I don't know why Aunt Fanny's so upset," Charlotte declared defensively. "Ruthie looks very cute. In my opinion, it's very attractive, and very original. Some people just have no idea what real beauty is."

"Real beauty!" Mama snapped. "Aunt Fanny says Ruthie's hair is so chopped up, she looks like a shorn sheep. She's ashamed to show her before people. Whatever gave you the notion in the first place? Aunt Fanny wanted you over there to mind Ruthie, not to be barbers!"

"First of all, Mama, don't blame Gertie," Charlotte said. "She had nothing to do with it. It was me. . . ."

22

Mama paced up and down. "But why? Whatever possessed you?"

"Well, Ruthie's hair was flopping into her eyes all the time. It was positively disgraceful! So I decided to do her a big favor and cut her bangs so she wouldn't get cross-eyed. And also, to enhance her beauty at the same time."

Henny spiraled a finger alongside her head. "Charlotte with her fanciful ideas!"

"It was a great idea!" Gertie carried on for Charlotte. "Only for some reason, it just kept coming out lopsided. Charlotte only tried to even it out. So . . ." Gertie lifted her shoulders, at a loss for further words.

"But to cut it all off!" Mama exploded. "I never heard of such a thing in my entire life!"

"In *Little Women,* Jo cut her hair off to sell it for money," Charlotte volunteered.

Henny tittered. "What are you going to do? Start selling hair for a living?"

Mama shook her head. "Oh, Charlotte, if I thought for one moment that you did this bad thing deliberately, you'd get from Papa the worst licking you ever got in your whole life! Now you go right in and telephone Aunt Fanny and apologize!"

Charlotte blanched. "Now?"

"Now!" commanded Mama.

Charlotte moved toward the telephone on dragging feet, with Gertie trailing after her. Slowly she gave the operator Aunt Fanny's phone number. Soon her aunt's voice, loud and irate, came buzzing over the wire. Charlotte listened meekly. When finally Aunt Fanny paused for breath, she began, "I'm sorry. . . ." But the angry buzzing had already resumed.

"I'm sorry, Aunt Fanny. . . ." Charlotte tried again, but the buzzing went right on.

Charlotte kept looking helplessly at Gertie. After what seemed an eternity, Gertie heard her say contritely, "All right, Aunt Fanny, no more hair-cutting, I promise!"

She raised her hand as if Aunt Fanny could see her. "And you know what, Aunt Fanny? I won't take any more money for staying with Ruthie until her hair grows back, no matter how long it takes!"

3

Election in the Balance

Rose plunked down her lunch tray and slid in among the knot of girls seated around a school cafeteria table. "Election for term representative to the General Organization is just a week away. Who's getting your vote?"

Lolly spooned up the last remaining beans on her plate. "I don't know. Who's running?"

"There are three candidates this time—Calvin Spencer . . ."

"Oh, the good-looking one with curly hair and beautiful eyes," Hannah gushed.

"Yes," agreed Henny, "but he's awfully stuck on himself. Thinks he's God's gift to women."

"Still you've got to admit he's great fun in class," Betty said. "He's always coming up with some wisecrack."

Henny dismissed Calvin with a flip of her hand. "Aw, he's just a big show-off. Who are the other two?"

"Jack Berger, the bean pole with the long nose—and Dennis Reilly. You know, the one whose ears stick out."

"Yeh," Henny grinned, "one look at him and you can tell which way the wind blows."

The girls burst into hysterics.

"Not much of a choice," Jenny remarked. "Not that it matters which one gets elected. It would still be a boy."

Rae nodded. "And with a boy representative to the

General Organization, most of the activities and programs are always planned for boys."

"So why don't we get a girl to run for a change?" Henny suggested.

"A girl!" the others chorused.

"Sure. Why not? Why does it always have to be a boy?" Henny looked around at the startled faces. "What's the matter? Don't you think a girl could handle the job?"

"I guess she could," Bessie considered. "It's just that we never thought of it before."

"I'm with you, Henny," Rose cried. "I think it's a great idea! Let's try. Even if we don't win, at least they'll realize girls have some rights after all."

"Who says we can't win? Don't forget the boys will have to split their votes three ways, while we'll have only one candidate." Henny was getting increasingly enthusiastic. "And if we can get all the girls to pull together, we stand a very good chance of winning."

"That's right," Mary broke in. "Who'll we nominate?"

"Henny, of course," Rose replied immediately.

"Wait a minute!" protested Henny. "Why me?"

"Because you'd be just perfect!" Rae burst out.

"Besides, it was your idea," Mary went on. She turned to the others. "Henny's a great debater. When it comes to an argument, nobody can equal her."

"Sure!" Lolly seized on the suggestion. "She's just like quicksilver. Try to catch her on one point and she's off like a shot on another. She could hold her own against any one of those candidates!"

By now everyone was sold on the idea. "Henny, you've got to do it!" they coaxed. "We need you."

"As term representative," Jenny tempted, "you'll get to

26

arrange the athletic events. You'll have to go out with the teams every time they play against some other high school. Think of all the boys you'll get to meet!"

"You're marvelous in gym," Lolly piped up. "Who knows? Maybe they'll even let you play on their basketball team."

The girls all ha-ha-ed at such a fanciful notion. When the merriment had subsided, Rose continued her urging. "Come on, Henny, what do you say?"

Any lingering doubts Henny might have had were slipping away. She felt a heady excitement at the challenge. "Okay, I'll do it!" she declared. "But I'm going to need lots of help."

"You'll get it!" everyone promised.

"We'll have to work fast," Henny continued. "Remember we've only got a week for campaigning." She was agog with ideas. "We're going to need lots of posters to hang up. And lots of leaflets to hand out. We'll have to enlist the help of the art kids to draw them for us."

"Henny, you're marvelous!" Hannah whooped. "The boys are going to get the surprise of their lives."

Lolly thought a moment. "I've got it! The first thing we've got to do is challenge our opponents to a debate. That'll give our candidate a real chance to shine!"

Mary laughed gleefully. "Boy, this is going to be some fun!"

At home everyone was amused over Henny's running for office, except possibly Papa. "Listen to her! A regular suffragette already! Next thing you know, she'll be marching in a parade carrying a sign like all those crazy women."

"They're not crazy, Papa," Henny retorted.

Papa shook his head doubtfully. "I feel sorry for our

27

country. What's going to happen when the women start taking over?"

"It might even be better," Mama returned mildly.

Papa clapped a hand to his head in mock horror. "Mama, you too?"

"Why not? Mama's a woman," Ella said. "Equal rights for women. It's coming, Papa. You can't stop it. Pretty soon the Suffrage Amendment is going to be submitted to the states. I bet by next year, women will have the right to vote."

Papa looked around at his family. "Charlie, with six suffragettes surrounding us, you and I don't stand a chance." His voice sounded woebegone, but his eyes were twinkling.

"The only thing, Henny," Mama added as an afterthought, "you're already so busy with your Social Club and your boyfriends, you pay little enough attention to your schoolwork now. What's going to happen when you have even less time to spare for your lessons?"

"Aw Ma, what are you worried about? I get passing marks."

"Just about," Mama acknowledged. "But I'm never quite sure you're going to make it."

"I'll make it all right, you'll see. And just think of all the fun I'm going to have meeting lots of new boys," Henny cried, smiling mischievously.

When the campaign first got under way, the boys treated it as some kind of joke. "The charge of the Suffragette Brigade," Calvin yelled, as the girls began putting up posters.

"That's just what we need around here, a girl rep," Jack Berger's gang jeered. "Instead of a baseball game, she could organize a sewing bee. Wouldn't that be just dandy?"

As for Reilly's supporters, they went around yelling:

> *Petticoat Lane*
> *Gives me a pain.*

The jibes only made the girls redouble their efforts. Every possible moment was spent lining up the girls and even corralling every boy who was willing to listen.

As election day neared, the boys began to play rough. They defaced the girls' signs with scribbles and daubs of paint. They handed out leaflets with statements like "How about it, boys? Do you want to join a cooking class?" Posters Henny's campaigners pinned up in the morning were found lying crumpled and torn on the floor by midday. Even the attractive poster outside their homeroom door was not spared. The pretty girl's face on it was disfigured by a large black walrus moustache. Underneath someone had penned, "Henrietta, the Suffragette."

"Those horrible boys!" Lolly stormed. "I could kill them for this!"

"Forget it," Henny told her. "It just proves they're getting scared."

"Okay, so they're scared," Hannah snapped. "But how can we go on running a campaign when they're constantly interfering with us?"

"Never mind. There's still the big debate tomorrow," Rose reminded her. "There they'll have to meet us on equal ground. It's all up to you now, Henny."

"I'll do my best," Henny responded with a confident grin.

Actually she was more anxious than she cared to admit. Her speech was ready. She'd worked hard over it, then tried it out on Ella and Sarah and felt encouraged when they had pronounced it good. But then one never knew what might happen during the rebuttal period.

Late afternoon the day of the debate, all the students were assembled in the auditorium. On stage right, Henny, seated beside her campaign manager, Rose, looked across uneasily to the empty chairs on the other side. It was getting late. Where were her opponents?

"I don't get it," she murmured to Rose. "I have a feeling that something's up."

The audience was growing restive. Soon cries of impatience and scattered applause began echoing through the room. "Come on! Let's get going!"

"Where are those boys?" Lolly demanded. "Why don't they show up?"

"Maybe we've scared them off," ventured Jenny.

Finally the teacher in charge of the debate said to Rose, "We'd better not wait any longer or the audience will start leaving. Your opponents will just have to lose the debate by default."

"All right," Rose agreed. She stood up. "Fellow students," she began, raising her hand for attention.

She never got it. All at once there came the sound of scuffling feet, buzzings, and sudden exclamations. Hilarious guffaws punctuated the air. What was going on?

Necks craned toward the rear of the auditorium. There stood the missing candidates dressed in regulation girls' gym bloomers, navy blue and puffed-out pleats! At a signal, they linked arms and came marching down the center aisle with Calvin holding aloft a poster proclaiming in big black letters, "We are the fighting Suffragettes!"

Up the steps of the stage they stomped, grimacing and tittering in silly-girl fashion. Bowing clumsily, Calvin thrust the poster into an astonished Rose's hands. Then the three turned their backs on the audience and—*allez oop!* —each executed a handstand. Their skinny legs projected comically from the bulky bloomers as they teetered unsteadily on their hands. It sent waves of laughter bouncing from wall to wall.

Utterly taken aback, Henny stood by numbly. She must do something! She could not let them get away with this. But what? Then in a flash, it came to her! Today was gym day. What a lucky break!

She picked up her schoolbag and dashed off into the wings. Yanking out her own gym bloomers from the bag, she ripped off her skirt and slipped them on. She was back on stage in a jiffy.

By now the three boys were throwing kisses to the audience and looking mighty pleased with themselves at the commotion they had caused.

Pushing past them, Henny strode to the front of the stage. She put two fingers to her lips and blew a loud, piercing whistle. Instantly, the audience quieted down, wondering what was going to happen next.

"Fellow students," Henny shouted, "this was supposed to be a debate. But if this is the only kind of argument my opponents can come up with, then let 'em try this!"

Whereupon she executed three perfect cartwheels across the stage floor. Then going into a handstand, she gracefully flipped over backward, landing quietly and smoothly

31

upright on her feet. Arms outstretched, she curtsied gracefully. A roar of approval rose from the audience.

For a moment, the boys were nonplussed. Then beanpole Jack also attempted a cartwheel. It was done so awkwardly that he knocked over a chair, bumping into his companions so that all three tangled in a heap. The result was that this time everyone appeared to be laughing *at* them rather than with them.

"You see," Henny pointed triumphantly at the crestfallen three. "They tried to turn this meeting upside down and look where they landed!" She pointed to her own feet. "But what we need is a representative with *understanding*."

At which the whole audience, girls and boys, stood up and cheered. "Henny! Henny! Yea, Henny!"

The day after election, Calvin, Jack, and Dennis approached the table in the cafeteria where Henny's friends were gathered.

"Where's our new General Organization rep?" they inquired.

"She's around somewhere," Jenny replied, warily.

"That Henny sure is a tough gal to beat," Calvin admitted grudgingly.

Rose laughed. "Well, she always was a whiz in gymnastics."

"Still, we did have a lot of fun," Jack said.

"We did," Rose agreed. "Only thing I'm sorry about though is that we never did get down to a serious discussion."

"What about?" demanded Calvin.

"Well you fellers have to get smart. You don't know what girls are like today," Rose replied. "Remember, when the war was on and there was a great need for workers, women moved right in on the job—in offices, hospitals, factories—every place we can think of." Her voice got louder and louder. "Now that the war is over, you can't send us back to the kitchen!"

"That's right," Hannah rushed in. "When women get the right to vote, they'll run for public office, too!"

"What do you girls want? A female president?" growled Calvin.

"Give us one reason why not?" Rose demanded.

Calvin backed off. "Okay. We'll argue about that some other time. Here!" He thrust an envelope at Rose. "Give this to Henny!"

Later Henny read the note to the girls.

We were fools when we decided to act like fools.
So we got fooled!
Congratulations on your victory.

> Calvin Spencer
> Jack Berger
> Dennis Reilly

"Well," Henny said with a bright smile, "it proves they're good sports after all."

4

The Letter

"No—no!" Professor Calvano insisted. "You're still singing from the throat! Push the voice up! The tone must come through the head!"

He put his fingers through his wiry hair so that it stood up like bristles on an angry porcupine.

"Listen!" Bouncing up from the piano stool like a jack-in-the-box, he flung back his head and put his left hand on his chest. Mouth open wide, he sang, "Aah," his right arm meanwhile describing a slow circle. The note swelled till it resounded throughout the parlor.

He hopped back onto the stool, his fingers poised over the piano keys. "Now you!" he ordered.

Ella's brow furrowed. The correct posture, the proper breath deep from the diaphragm, keeping the voice in the front of the mouth—the clear pronunciation of the foreign words. It was just plain hard work! But she did so love the opera arias. When she managed to sing even a single line without error, that was pure joy. She tried once again.

Professor Calvano shook his head doubtfully. "Well—so, so. Take a rest, then we do it some more."

Ella's spirits dampened. Slumped in her chair, she watched the professor riffling through a pile of music. What a nervous, jittery person! But he's really a marvelous teacher. He works so hard with me. These last two years I've made a lot of progress, I know. I can feel it. I look forward to my lessons. Dread them, too. He can be pretty frightening the way he's always demanding the best from me. If he doesn't get it, he grows furious, making sarcastic remarks till I feel completely crushed.

She sighed. It isn't always easy to do one's best. Especially after a long, dreary day at the office. If only I could devote all my time to just music, what progress I could make. Well, what's the use even thinking about it? I have to work, else how could I pay for my lessons?

Gosh, I'm hungry. I wonder what Mama has for dinner.

"All right," Professor Calvano broke into her thoughts. "Sing now the aria from *The Bohemian Girl*."

Fatigue miraculously effaced, hunger forgotten, she sang the song she so dearly loved:

> *As through the streets*
> *I wandered onward merrily . . .*

Her voice emerged clear, the tone velvet smooth, the high notes taken with ease.

"Stop! Stop!" Professor Calvano yelled. He covered his ears and shook his head from side to side in agony. "I can't stand it!"

Ella halted abruptly, a look of pain crossing her face. "What did I do wrong?" she asked.

"It's not you! You were good—very good! It's that dog."

"Dog?" Ella repeated.

"You mean you didn't hear him?" her teacher exclaimed.

"No. I was so busy trying to sing correctly, I didn't hear anything."

35

"My God! Every time you hit a high note, the dog howled. If you own a dog, do you have to allow him to sit right outside the door when I'm giving a lesson?"

"But Professor," Ella put in timidly, "we don't own a dog."

"You're telling me I don't know what I hear?" snapped the professor. "I'll prove it to you. Sing me a high C."

Ella did as she was told and sure enough this time she heard it too—an unmistakable mournful howl.

"It must be Prince, the Healys' dog. They live downstairs," Ella explained apologetically.

She opened the parlor door just in time to see Prince scampering down the stairs with Charlie. "Charlie!" Ella called after him. Too late! Boy and dog had disappeared.

"That Charlie! Will I give it to him," she muttered.

"Well, it's already late," the professor announced. "We finish for today. Practice your scales, and remember—next time, please, no dog!"

By the time Ella came into the dining room, the table had already been cleared. Papa, puffing away at his pipe, was seated as usual in the morris chair, immersed in his newspaper. Charlie was curled up on the leather couch, a finger moving slowly across the page of a primer as he mouthed the words.

"Charlie, I'm very angry at you! Why did you do it?"

Ella had shouted so loudly, it brought Mama, Henny, and Sarah in from the kitchen.

"What happened?" Mama asked.

"You know what he did? He brought Prince up here and put him by the parlor door so he would set up a howl every time I tried to sing." Ella turned on the little boy. "You know very well I'm not to be disturbed when I'm

36

taking a lesson. Professor Calvano was so annoyed, he left in a huff!"

"But I didn't bring him up," Charlie protested. "Honest, Ella, he came up by himself."

"The door downstairs must have been open again," Mama suggested.

"I heard him sniffling about," Charlie continued, "so I went out and that's when I found him standing by the parlor door. You know, Ella, he was singing! He was having such a good time, I couldn't chase him away."

Gertie giggled. "Prince was taking a lesson from the professor."

"And for free, too," added Henny.

"I wonder why they don't write music for a talented dog," Charlotte remarked.

Everyone laughed. Papa shook his head. "There goes my daughter Charlotte again with her imagination."

"I think Prince was real good," Charlie said. "Maybe not as good as you, Ella."

"Thanks," Ella replied. "That's what I call a real compliment." But she couldn't resist a smile amid the general merriment.

"Well, it better not happen again," she warned. "I'll have to ask Mr. Healy to keep Prince downstairs—at least on my lesson night. Professor Calvano won't stand for it."

Mama waved a hand. "Enough already. Henny and Sarah, finish washing the dishes. Ella, sit down and eat. You must be hungry."

"I'm starved!"

"Oh, by the way, I almost forgot. A letter came for you today." Mama rummaged in her apron pocket. "It's from Cousin Nathan."

37

"Cousin Nathan? Why should he be writing to me?"

Henny peered over Ella's shoulder. "Let's read the letter and find out."

"Henny, please!" Ella clasped the letter to her chest. "It just might happen to be personal."

Henny flipped the dish towel. "Personal! Hah!"

"I can hardly recall what Cousin Nathan looks like," Sarah remarked. "But I do remember that he played the violin like a dream. How long is it since he went to live in Albany, Mama?"

"I'd say about five years, Sarah. He runs a very successful music school there."

"Oh, listen to this, everybody!" Ella burst out. She read aloud:

Dear Cousin Ella,

Last week I happened to meet Professor Calvano and he told me what wonderful progress you were making. Our Community Center here is planning a concert for the first Sunday afternoon in April and I was wondering if you'd like to take part in it. It would mean singing three or four numbers. They'd pay you $10.00 and also your travel expenses.

If you decide to come, you could take the Albany night boat on Saturday evening. That would bring you here in time for rehearsal Sunday morning.

You will have to stay over in Albany Sunday night but that is no problem. You will be put up in the same boardinghouse where I live. My landlady runs a very clean and comfortable place and she says she'd be more than happy to accommodate you.

Let me know if you can come. You'll have a fine time. There'll be a party and a dance after the concert.

Remember me to your father and mother, to all your sisters and little brother.

Your loving cousin,
Nathan

P.S. By the way, if you have a nice photograph of yourself, please send it right away. We'll need it for publicity.

Ella stared down at the letter. "Can you imagine that Professor Calvano! He never even mentioned a word to me!"

"It's marvelous!" exclaimed Charlotte. "Imagine singing in a regular concert!"

"It's just a small local affair," Ella said, but her eyes sparkled.

"It's certainly nice of Nathan to ask you," Mama observed.

"And why shouldn't he ask her?" Papa exclaimed. "If your own family won't do anything for you, who will?"

"Are you lucky!" Henny cried. "Nobody in this family ever gets to go anywhere. Now here you are, traveling all the way up to the state capital! Why don't you find out if they need a dancer so I can go along?" Cocking her head to one side, she added teasingly, "By the way, what's your boyfriend going to say about your running off for the weekend?"

Two little flags of pink appeared on Ella's cheeks. "He'll be proud as can be," she flashed back. But for a moment her joy was clouded over. *I won't be able to see Jules* for almost the whole weekend! If only he could come along . . .

She folded the letter and put it back into its envelope. "I'll answer it right after I eat."

Mama rushed to the stove. "Here we've been so busy talking and you haven't had a bite to eat yet."

5

Albany Dream

A final roaring blast and the Albany night boat slid slowly away from the dock. Pressed tight against the rail, amid the crowd of passengers, Ella kept fluttering her handkerchief in farewell to Jules and her family.

Everyone seemed to be spilling over with joy for her, everyone, that is, but Jules. There was something about his manner, as if he resented her departure. Why should he be upset? she wondered. She'd only be away for the weekend.

Gradually the boat picked up speed. Soon the figures of all her dear ones diminished and disappeared into the distance. Still she lingered, till all was melted into the darkness.

Later, in her tiny cabin, she started to unpack her night things. The gentle rolling of the boat was not unpleasant— the steady pulse of the engines, the creaking of wood. But what was this other sound? Singing? She listened intently. It was singing! Where was it coming from? She must find out.

She made her way upstairs to the main deck, the singing growing more distinct with every step. They were men's voices, singing in perfect harmony. A professional group? They certainly sounded like it.

41

The salon was thronged with passengers. Ella edged her way through, and her amazed eyes fell upon a group of porters, wearing uniforms of red caps and white jackets. Standing in a neat row, they were singing a familiar spiritual in rich, resonant voices. She moved in closer. She couldn't resist singing along softly.

One of the basses smiled at the sound of her voice and beckoned to her to join in.

Ella needed no second invitation. As if of its own accord, her mouth opened and her clear soprano soared forth.

The porters eyed one another in approval and opened rank to make room for her. The audience, delighted by this unexpected turn, craned their necks the better to see this small young girl whose pure high voice mingled so enchantingly with the male voices.

The song's end brought a round of applause. "My, such a lovely voice!" people were exclaiming. "So powerful too! Where does it come from? She's so tiny."

Flushing with pleasure, Ella felt nonetheless a bit uneasy. Had she stolen the limelight? She started apologizing. "I really didn't mean to barge in. But it was so hard to resist. You're all so wonderful!"

"Thank you, miss," the man who seemed to be the leader replied. "You're pretty wonderful yourself."

"That's the way it is if you're a singer," one of the other porters said. "You just gotta sing along. Do you know 'Swing Low, Sweet Chariot'?"

"Yes."

"Good! It's our next number."

Song followed song with the audience in rapt attention.

Ella was in seventh heaven. How like a miracle it was to be suddenly made part of such a magnificent choir!

"Well, folks, there's time for just one more number," the leader announced. He took off his hat and held it out invitingly as he made his way through the audience.

The final song was being sung as hands dug into pockets and handbags. And as the coins fell clinking into the hat, the singing speeded up and the smiles on the singers' faces grew wider and wider.

"That's all, folks. Thank you kindly."

The porters doffed their hats in unison and bowed.

The crowd was beginning to disperse when Ella felt a tap on her shoulder. "Just a minute, miss. We have decided," the leader said, "that since you were part of our performance tonight, you share in the pot."

"Oh no," Ella protested. "It's very generous, but really I couldn't! I had such a marvelous time, I ought to pay you for allowing me to join in."

"Well, if that's the way you want it. But it was a great pleasure."

"With that kind of an arrangement," one of the other porters joked, "you're welcome anytime—anytime at all."

Ella laughed heartily. "I'll have to think it over. Good night to you all."

She strolled out of the salon onto the open deck. Faces turned toward her with such open admiration, it made her feel as if she were walking on air.

The wind whipped by, flapping her coat against her ankles. She pushed forward, inhaling deeply the strong steady stream of air. Grasping hold of the rail, she stood still a moment, feeling suddenly very much alone in the immensity of sky and water expanding before her. Along the darkened far-off shore loomed the cliffs of the Palisades dotted here and there with a twinkle of light. She thought of the legend of the little people who inhabited this shadowed valley, and the game of bowls they had played with Rip Van Winkle. Tomorrow morning, she too would waken to another world—just like Rip.

Tomorrow—her thoughts switched to the coming event. Would the audience in Albany respond to her the way her fellow passengers had? In a way, tonight's performance was like a rehearsal. It's bound to be different at a real concert where people have bought tickets. She shook off the creeping doubt. If Professor Calvano hadn't thought I was good enough, Cousin Nathan wouldn't have asked me in the first place.

Cousin Nathan—*there* was an example of what discipline and hard work could achieve. His parents were very poor. He had to wait until he went to work at sixteen before he could even begin studying the violin. All those years he scrimped and saved to pay for his lessons. And every night, after a long hard working day, he'd practice. Hour after hour, with a mute on his instrument so the neighbors would not be disturbed. But he had never considered he was making any sacrifice because he loved music so passionately. Now music was his whole life. I wonder—could it be my whole life, too?

Just a little further along the railing, a couple stood close together. Ella felt a quick pang of loneliness. If only Jules were here.

For a while she stared down at the water churning in a long furrow. She shivered a little, chilled by the wind and cold. Retracing her steps, she went down to her little cabin.

44

The engines stilled. The boat floated quietly toward the dock. For a moment all was serene. But then the sudden jar of the boat against the pilings, the shouts of the deckhands, the roll of the gangway being trundled out, the screams of gulls overhead, the fitful roar of the wind, and the reverse of engines, all struck up a symphony of sound—the music of arrival.

Ella scanned the city unfolding before her. The spire of a church steeple reached high out of the morning grayness. Tall and proud it surmounted the assorted rows of dark boxlike buildings that lined the riverbank.

Albany may be the state's capital, she thought, but the skyline is certainly unimpressive. There's nothing here like our Woolworth Building.

Ella could see a score of people gathered on the landing. Would she be able to pick out Nathan? After all, it's been five years. Was he still the handsome bachelor? Odd he'd never married.

Someone was calling her name. There! There he was! She waved excitedly.

Suitcase bumping against her side, she hurried down the gangplank. Nathan came forward to greet her.

"Ella, how are you?" He smiled, his mouth wide and generous, just like Papa's.

"Why you're a young lady," Nathan exclaimed. "Lucky for me you sent your picture or I'd never have recognized you."

Ella smiled. "I had to grow up sometime."

"True," he replied. "Did you enjoy the trip?"

"Oh yes. It was just heavenly."

"Good. Let's get going. We'll have just enough time to get you settled before rehearsal."

45

They boarded a streetcar. As it wound its way slowly through the heart of the city, Ella kept turning from side to side trying to take everything in. She was vaguely disappointed. She hadn't really known what to expect, but somehow Albany seemed small-townish to her. Row upon row of low buildings, dull-looking factories, people moving unhurriedly through the narrow streets. There seemed to be none of the excitement she felt back home. But a little further on, she noticed the neighborhood had begun to improve.

"That's the state capitol." Nathan pointed to a huge building, fronted by a seemingly endless flight of stairs. "That's where all the state's laws are made."

Swaying and bumping along, the streetcar soon sped away from the town's center into a more residential area. A few minutes later they had arrived at the old brownstone house where Nathan lived. Ella followed the plump landlady up the carpeted stairs to a small but attractive room on an upper floor. Quickly she unpacked and put away her things.

"My that was fast!" Nathan declared when she came tripping down the stairs. "The Community Center is just a few blocks away from here. We'll be right on time."

The rehearsal proceeded smoothly. When it was over, the piano accompanist said, "You may be tiny, but oh my, there's nothing tiny about your voice. Your singing will round out our instrumental program perfectly."

Afterward Nathan took her to lunch at a little café nearby. The small tables and soft rose lighting gave the place a cozy atmosphere. The owner welcomed Nathan warmly. When introduced to Ella, he gave her an especially big smile and waved toward the cashier's desk.

46

There on the wall for all to see, hung a large poster with the caption, "The little girl with the big voice!"

"Why—it's me!" Ella gasped.

Nathan chuckled. "How do you like your billing?"

"I don't know," she faltered. "Oh Nathan, how, can I live up to that? It's so—so professional. I'm scared!"

"Of course you are. Everybody is before a performance." He patted her arm comfortingly. "You'll be fine. Once you're onstage, the nervousness will go. You'll see."

"I hope so," Ella said, smiling wanly.

"Good luck!" someone whispered. Someone else smiled and pressed her hand. Someone even kissed her lightly on the check. Was it Nathan? And there she was—onstage confronting a sea of upturned faces.

There was a scattered round of applause. Ella suddenly felt buoyant. Why, they want to like me. They're telling me not to worry—to go ahead and sing. At once she was filled with the desire to return the warmth and friendliness flowing up to her.

The introductory bars were being played. Ella took a deep breath and her voice floated free and light as a bird on the wing.

With each song, her confidence grew. She was singing well. She could feel it. It turned out that the numbers she had come prepared to sing were not enough. The audience clamored for more. So she sang her final encore over again.

Afterward, Ella stood backstage amid the other performers, with Nathan at her side, shaking hands and acknowledging compliments. This was the reward for all her hard work and constant practice. Oh, but it's worth it—every bit of it, she exulted.

At the fringe of the crowd surrounding her, there hovered a paunchy, moon-faced man wearing steel-rimmed glasses and a high, stiff collar, clutching a derby in his hand. Only when the crowd had thinned out did he approach her.

"Young lady," he said, "you're quite a warbler."

"Thank you, sir."

"You an Albany girl?"

"No. I'm from New York City."

He nodded. "Is that so? You interested in the big time?"

"Big time?" Ella repeated.

Nathan laughed. "He means the professional stage."

The stranger did not wait for her answer. "Well now, don't misunderstand," he continued. "I'm not a talent scout. As a matter of fact, I'm the manager of the vaudeville theatre here. But I've got a friend, Mr. Hart, and he's a scout for the top producers on Broadway. My friend's going to audition in a couple of weeks. If you're interested, I'll be glad to let him, or your manager here, know."

"I'm not her manager. She's just my cousin," Nathan explained. "I live here in Albany. He'd have to contact her folks in New York."

The stranger copied down Ella's address and phone number. "Well, you'll be hearing from him," he promised. "You were swell, young lady. Good luck."

Clapping his derby on his head, he turned on his heel and was gone.

Startled by the unexpected development, Ella could only look to Nathan and ask, "What do you think?"

48

Nathan put up a restraining hand. "You mustn't put too much stock in this kind of offer. If he calls, okay. If not, don't let it bother you."

"Oh Nathan, I feel as if I were in a dream. . . . I hope I never wake up!"

6

Charlie Meets Elijah

Ella sat curled up in a big armchair downstairs in the Healy flat.

"You know, Grace," she mused, "it's only two weeks since I came home from Albany and already the whole thing seems like something that never really happened."

"It's always that way when you go off somewhere and then return home," Grace responded.

Ella heaved a sigh of content. "It's so heavenly peaceful down here. I love my family—every single one of them—but sometimes it gets so noisy in our apartment, you can't hear yourself think. Honestly, sometimes I almost wish I were an only child, like you."

Grace shook her head vigorously. "Oh no you don't. You can't possibly imagine how lonely it can be. I think big families are great. I'd trade with you anytime. When I get married, I want to be knee-deep in children." Her eyes met Ella's and she laughed a little. "Here I am talking about marriage and no one's even asked me yet."

Ella looked at her sympathetically. "Have you any idea when Bill's coming home?" she asked. "After all, the war ended about six months ago."

"His last letter said soon. I had hoped it would be by Easter. I even bought a whole new Easter outfit. I keep thinking how wonderful it would be—the four of us, you and Jules, Bill and me—all together again." Her shoulders lifted helplessly. "But I guess we'll just have to wait."

She turned toward Ella with an appealing gesture. "When I think of seeing Bill again, I am so overwhelmed with happiness, I can hardly bear it. . . ." Her voice trailed off.

Sweet, lovely Grace, reflected Ella, with her vision of the future so simple and clear—marriage, love, children and Bill. No yearning for something more, the way it is with me. Does it mean that I love Jules any the less? Or is it that I am incapable of loving anyone completely as Grace does? That man in Albany. He didn't promise anything. But still I can't help keep thinking about it and hoping his friend will call.

"Ella," Grace called her back to the here and now, "don't you just love Easter? It comes at the nicest time of the year."

Ella nodded. "Just like Passover. Which reminds me, Mama said to be sure and invite you to our Seder. Will you come?"

"I'd love to."

It was late afternoon on the eve of Passover. The house looked particularly clean and tidy. As was customary, all the dishes and pots used during the rest of the year had been put away. Now the table was laid with the china and glassware reserved especially for use throughout the Passover week. The old morris chair, piled high with cushions, was moved to the head of the table. Tonight when the family celebrated the Seder service, Papa, dressed in his white ceremonial robe and skullcap embroidered in gold, would recline in the chair like a king. In like manner, Jews all over the world would celebrate their deliverance from the land of Egypt.

Meanwhile in the kitchen, Charlie watched Papa lay out the symbolic foods on the large Seder plate.

"Will Elijah come to our house again tonight, Papa?" he asked.

"Certainly. Elijah comes to the Seder every year."

"Does he go to everybody's house?"

"Yes."

"All over the world?"

"Yes, Charlie."

"But how can he get around so fast?"

"Why, with four strokes of his mighty wings, Elijah can cover the whole world! No place is too far away for him."

Charlie mulled this over for a moment. Then he came out with "Papa, at the end of the Seder, when we open the door for Elijah to come in to drink the wine from his own cup, why can't we see him?"

"Because he makes himself invisible. But even so, we can feel that he is there and we're glad he has come to bless our house and all the people in it."

Charlie still wasn't satisfied. "But why does he make himself invisible?"

Papa smiled. "Well, that's the way angels behave sometimes. Charlie, did you know that once, a long, long time ago, Elijah lived on earth?"

Charlie's eyes became round as marbles. "He did?"

"Yes, he really did. In those days he was a prophet in the kingdom of Israel. Everyone loved him because he was so good and kind. He helped all the poor people and punished the wicked ones. When he died it was said that he went straight up to heaven in a fiery chariot.

"But though Elijah now lives in heaven, he has never forgotten his people. He has come back to earth many times, performing miracles to protect someone in danger or to help someone in great trouble. There are lots and lots of stories about him."

"Could you tell me one, Papa?"

"Well, one story tells how Elijah comes to the home of a poor man and his wife and asks for something to eat. They invite him in to share their food even though there is hardly enough for themselves. But the moment Elijah sits down at the table, lo and behold, lots of good things to eat suddenly appear!

"The poor people are overcome with joy. Elijah smiles and is gone!

"Later Elijah knocks on the gate of a rich man and begs for shelter. But the rich man is mean and selfish. 'Go away!' he says. 'I have no room for beggars!'

"Elijah turns away but he leaves behind a terrible misfortune. The rich man loses all his money!"

"Didn't they know it was Elijah?" Charlie asked.

"No. All the legends say that no one ever recognizes Elijah. He always wears some kind of disguise."

"I wish I could see him."

"Who knows, Charlie? Maybe you will someday. Maybe you have seen him already, but you don't know it." Papa patted him on the head. "I remember another story about a boy like you who also wanted to see Elijah. Would you like to hear it?"

"Oh yes!"

"Well," began Papa, "once there was a very famous rabbi. When this rabbi was still a young boy, he wanted to

53

see Elijah the Prophet very much. So he begged his father to show Elijah to him.

"The boy's father said, 'If you study the Torah very hard, maybe then you will be worthy of seeing him.'

"The boy studied hard, day and night. At the end of a year, he said to his father, 'Papa, I did just what you told me. I've studied the Torah very hard, but still Elijah has not shown himself to me.'

"So the boy's father answered, 'You are too impatient, my son. When Elijah thinks you really deserve it, he'll show himself to you.'

"One night, when the young boy was studying all alone in his father's synagogue, an old man came in. His clothes were torn and dirty-looking, and held together with a rope tied around his middle. He was carrying a heavy sack on his back. His tired, wrinkled face was not very clean either. All in all, I can tell you, he wasn't a very pleasant sight.

"He didn't say anything. He just plopped the sack down on the floor and slumped down beside it, right there in the synagogue!

"This made the boy angry. 'What do you mean settling yourself here?' he yelled at the old man. 'This is not an inn where you get a night's lodging.'

" 'I'm sorry,' the stranger said. 'I did not mean to dishonor the synagogue. But I'm so tired. Please, let me rest here for just a little while; then I'll be off.'

" 'No, you can't stay here!' the boy shouted. 'I'm sure my father wouldn't like to have tramps coming in here with their dirty things.'

"The poor old man sighed wearily. He staggered to his feet, picked up his heavy bundle and went away.

54

"A little while later, the boy's father returned to the synagogue. 'Well, my son,' he asked, 'have you seen Elijah yet?'

"The boy shook his head sadly. 'No, father, I haven't. All I saw was an old tramp with a sack on his back.'

" 'Did you welcome him with the words *Shalom aleichem* [Peace be with you]?' the father asked.

" 'No, father, I didn't,' the boy replied.

" 'Oh, my foolish son! Why didn't you? Didn't you know that that was Elijah?' Sorrowfully he shook his head. 'Alas, I'm afraid now it's too late.'

"From that day on, the young boy changed. He never failed to welcome anyone, no matter who he was, or how he looked. And Charlie," Papa held up a warning finger, "you must do the same."

Charlie dug his hands into his pockets and walked slowly to his room. The picture of the old man plodding along with a heavy sack on his back kept reappearing before him. There was something very familiar about it. What was it?

Then, like a dart of lightning, it came to him! Of course! Grabbing his jacket, he slipped out through the parlor door so quietly, no one noticed his going.

The sun had set. The guests were already assembled around the table. To the right of Papa's throne, were Uncle Hyman, Aunt Lena, Tanta, and Grace. To the left sat Aunt Fanny and Uncle Joe and Ruthie—looking a little less like a plucked chicken, now that her hair had grown out a little. All the other chairs were occupied by the family—all, that is, except one.

"Where's Charlie? All day long he could hardly wait for

55

the Seder to begin," Papa cried, annoyed. "Now where is he?"

"Charlie! Charlie!" the sisters called, running through the house searching everywhere—under beds, inside closets, behind the piano, and even out in the hall. No Charlie anywhere!

"He may have gone downstairs," Henny suggested. "I'll go look."

"We didn't see him when we came," Aunt Lena declared.

"We didn't see him either," Aunt Fanny added. "Tsk, tsk! What could have happened to the child?"

"Could he have gone to your house, Grace?" Mama asked, by now a bit worried.

Grace hurried toward the door. "I'll see."

In a few minutes both she and Henny were back. No Charlie!

"Could he have gone to a friend's house?" Ella offered.

Mama shook her head. "Tonight?"

"Where could he be?" everyone wondered out loud.

Papa was completely baffled. "He was in the kitchen with me just a little while ago. I was telling him a story. How was it no one saw him go?"

"We were all so busy with last-minute things, no one paid any attention," Sarah put in.

"Tonight of all nights!" Papa's voice rose angrily.

Aunt Lena signaled to Mama. "Why don't you call up one of his friends anyway?" she urged.

"Yes. Yes, I will." Mama started for the phone.

Precisely at that moment, the kitchen door was heard opening.

"Charlie?" Mama called out hopefully.

"Papa, Papa!" Charlie's voice sounded all excited.

"Charlie, where were you?" Papa cried. "Just when we are to begin the . . ." Papa's unfinished sentence hung in midair. Charlie was not alone. Behind him trailed a short, stocky man with graying hair, a mass of curls tumbling over his forehead. He was dressed in a faded brown shirt and baggy trousers held together by a rope tied around his middle. It was Tony, the iceman!

Taking hold of Tony's hand, Charlie propelled him gently forward. "See, Papa," he announced triumphantly, his face radiant with happiness, "I brought Elijah!"

Speechless, everyone eyed the unexpected guest. Finally, Aunt Fanny found her voice. "What kind of Elijah is this?" she tittered. "Tony, the iceman?"

"Could be," Tanta said. "After all, Elijah always carried a bundle on his back. And with Tony, it's always a sack of coal in the winter or a big block of ice in the summer."

Grins appeared on all the faces, but Papa shook his head disapprovingly. At once the grins disappeared.

"Excuse me," Tony said hastily, "your little Charlie, he tells me it is Seder night and I must come upstairs with him and drink the wine. I could not say no to the little boy. So I come."

Papa nodded and pointed to the wine bottle. "Help yourself, Tony."

Tony picked up the glass nearest him already filled.

"No, no Elijah," Charlie bounced up and down. "You have to drink from your own cup!"

Tony mussed the boy's hair. "That's all right, Charlie. This'll do fine." Without further ado, he drained the glass.

"Well, I thank you. The wine, it is good—very good. Now I must go. I still have some ice to deliver. Good night and a happy holiday to all of you."

As the door closed behind Tony, the glow faded from Charlie's face. Mournfully he looked at Elijah's cup on the table. He turned to Papa. "He didn't drink from his cup. I guess maybe it wasn't Elijah after all."

Papa put his arm around Charlie and drew him close.

"Well Charlie, we'll never know, will we? Maybe he didn't want to be recognized. Come, my son, take your place and let the Seder begin."

7

A Lucky Break

Returning home from work one evening, Ella was greeted by a beaming Mama with "There was a telephone call for you today!"

"Yes?"

"The friend of that man you met in Albany," Mama replied. "He said they're auditioning tomorrow morning, and if you're interested, you're to be there at ten o'clock sharp. You're to ask for a Mr. Trent. Here! I wrote down the address."

Mama's words caused an instant commotion among the girls. They surrounded Ella, all demanding to be heard.

"Are you really going to go?" "Will it be a real show on Broadway?" "Of course you're taking Mama!" "Can we go along?" "Will they make you a star?"

Ella covered her ears. "Please, everybody, don't all pounce on me at once! Give me a chance to think!"

For a brief moment, all was quiet. Then practical Sarah spoke up. "Ella, what about your job?"

"That's easy. She'll just take the day off," Henny declared. "A chance like this comes only once in a lifetime!"

There followed a spirited discussion as to what Ella should wear, how she should act, what she should sing. What she should say. Through it all, Ella was silent, her mind tossing back and forth on waves of elation and panic. It kept right on tossing a good part of the night.

Morning finally came. As usual, Papa set off for work and the children were dispatched to school. But for Ella it was an extra-special morning. With painstaking care, she groomed herself for the audition. She chose her best dress, a simple maroon wool with a white collar crossed demurely in front. A black hat with maroon facing topped off the costume.

Looking at her, Mama was infinitely touched. My first-born, she thought, young and eager. God grant she realizes her desire.

On her part, Ella was admiring her mother's still youthful figure dressed up in her best—her braid-trimmed frock. I'm so proud Mama looks so nice.

Arm in arm, mother and daughter left the house and walked the few blocks to the subway station.

The time seemed to drag along ever so slowly as the train rattled its way downtown. Then at long last they were in the heart of magical Times Square.

Armed with their precious slip of paper, they soon found themselves standing before an old brownstone building. Up several flights of wooden stairs they climbed, to the third floor.

From inside a succession of closed glass-paneled doors, streamed a bedlam of sound—pianos thumping, banjos strumming, and sudden snatches of song reverberating down the length of the corridor. Ella knocked on the door marked Foster Music Co.

"We might as well go in," Mama said after a few minutes of waiting. "Nobody can hear us in all this racket."

Timidly Ella turned the doorknob.

They entered a fairly large room, rather bare-looking. In one corner stood an upright piano piled high with sheet music. A man in shirt sleeves, a cigarette dangling from his lips, was tinkling the keys, his eyes intent on some music before him. Beside the piano, a thin longish-legged individual, wearing a cap tipped toward his nose, teetered on the hind legs of a cane chair. Near one of the long windows overlooking the street, a short, somewhat stocky man and a group of pretty girls were chatting and laughing familiarly. No one paid any attention to the newcomers.

For a few moments, Ella and Mama looked around uncertainly. Then Ella approached the group at the window.

"Mr. Trent?" she ventured.

The man turned. "Yep. I'm Mr. Trent," he said, glancing down at her. "What is it, little girl?"

Now all the girls were staring at her. Hastily, Ella introduced herself and Mama. "Your friend heard me sing in Albany."

"Oh, yeah, yeah." He motioned toward the piano player. "Just tell him what you want to sing and give him the key."

"I brought my music with me," Ella began. "Can I . . ."

"Sure, kid," he replied, his tone indifferent.

Ella unrolled her music. "It's 'The Flower Song' from *Faust*. Is that all right?"

Mr. Trent raised a quizzical eyebrow. Out of the corner of her eye, Ella could see some of the girls exchanging amused glances. Is there something wrong with my choice? she wondered. It's gay and charming. And I can sing it well. Her head lifted resolutely.

Mr. Trent pulled out a chair for Mama, then waved his hand matter-of-factly to Ella. "Okay, kid, let's hear it."

The pianist struck the opening chords and Ella started to sing. As her voice resounded through the room, she suddenly became aware of how quiet everyone had grown.

The thin man in the cane chair ceased his rocking. He pushed his cap back on his head. He leaned forward and his penetrating gaze seemed to be probing her very being.

Ella felt momentarily unnerved by his scrutiny but she kept herself in hand. You're not going to upset me, she challenged the ogling stranger. Who do you think you are anyway? Just you wait, and I'll show you. . . !

In a way his attention was flattering. To respond was irresistible. Soon she found herself singing especially for his benefit. She smiled, gestured coquettishly, the melody all the while lilting forth with ease and gaiety. At the finish, she curtsied, and stood waiting expectantly.

Without a word, the thin man rose, grabbed her by the arm and led her toward the door.

"My music . . ."

"Get it, Mother, and come along," he ordered.

Ella hung back. "But Mr. Trent," she appealed over her shoulder.

"It's okay, kid," Mr. Trent assured her with a broad smile. "That's Mr. Woods," as if the mere mention of the name was sufficient.

Before she knew it, she was out the door, down the stairs, and in the street. Up Broadway they raced, Ella running to keep up with Mr. Woods's long-legged stride, with Mama following in bewildered pursuit.

Mr. Woods led them down the block into another building. They rode up in an elevator and were ushered into an office. Ella had just time enough to read the gold lettering on the door—Joe Woods, Theatrical Agent. So that's what he is, she telegraphed to Mama as they went inside.

They found themselves in a large, square room with a receptionist seated at a desk facing the entrance. To one side, beneath a row of framed photographs, a number of men and women were seated. Upon Mr. Woods's entrance, they stood up in a body and pressed forward. He waved them back with an imperious gesture as he rushed past.

"I'm not to be disturbed," he called out to the receptionist, and conducted Mama and Ella into a smaller private room. The door swung shut behind them.

Skillfully, he tossed his cap onto a coat rack. "Sit down, please," he said, indicating the leather chairs on either side of the desk.

Leaning back in his chair, he rubbed a finger speculatively along the side of his nose, his shrewd eyes meanwhile measuring Ella. Somewhat flustered, she avoided his gaze and fell to contemplating her hands. Why doesn't he say something? she wondered.

Finally he spoke, addressing himself to Mama. "Your daughter has something. Something that's much more important than just good looks. Something that can get across to an audience, like an electric current. And that's what I'm always looking for." He turned toward Ella. "And with that big voice coming out of that little body, you've got it, little girl! And I want it!"

He spun around in his chair and pointed to the photographs hung on every side. "See those?" His arm swept out. "Stars, every one of them! And I made them! All of them! And I can make you, too!"

Ella felt her temples throbbing with excitement. Yesterday was only hope. Now it was a reality. Always the dream had shimmered like a rainbow. Why then did the fulfillment of the dream suddenly seem so terrifying? . . . Everything's happening so fast! I feel as if I were on a roller coaster. I'm all confused. I need time to think. She looked at Mama beseechingly. To her surprise Mama's eyes were glistening. She was taking in every word.

Mr. Woods tapped the ends of his long fingers together, all while studying Ella. "What's the matter?" he asked bluntly. "Don't you like what I'm telling you?"

Did her turmoil shown so plainly? Ella tried to compose herself. "Yes"—she faltered—"yes, I do."

He bent forward, jabbing the air with his finger. "Now listen, little girl." His voice took on an almost fatherly tone. "I said I want you. But that's not enough. You've got to want, too. You've got to want to be on the stage more than anything else in the whole world! Otherwise it's no good. No good at all! Understand?"

Ella nodded weakly.

He sat back and surveyed the ceiling. "Of course, right now, you're positively green. You need experience. The act Mr. Trent's putting together is just the ticket. It's a comedy act. It's called 'Nine Crazy Kids.' It's all about nine girls—those girls you saw, dressed up as schoolgirls, pestering their teacher. It'll be very bright and fast-moving with lots of singing and dancing. You'll work in that for a season out on the road. Then maybe you'll be ready for the kind of show I've got in mind."

He opened his desk drawer and brought out some forms. "I'm prepared to give you a contract right now. Of course you'll have to sign up with me exclusive—for five years."

Five years! Ella gulped. Her eyes sought Mama's. What should I say? she entreated silently. But Mama's face too was a jumble of emotions: wonder, pride, concern.

"You sign up with me, young lady," Mr. Woods went on, "and for a start, I'll get you thirty dollars a week. Not much maybe, but as I said, it's just for a start."

Not much! Ella caught her breath. Why, it's twice what I'm earning now!

"Of course, you'll have to pay your own expenses out of that while you're on the road. Not transportation. That's taken care of. But board and lodging will be your own responsibility. You can always team up with a couple of the girls. Save expenses that way. You'll make out all right. You don't strike me as one of those silly kids that'll blow all her dough."

He turned to Mama. "Mother, you gotta look at it this way. This year will be a training period. If she works hard and sticks by me, I promise that she'll go far. Very far."

A little while of silence and then Mama spoke. "Please, Mr. Woods, could we take the contract home with us? I'd like to talk it over with my husband."

"Sure, sure." He folded the contract, slipped it into an envelope, and handed it to Mama. "Rehearsals will not begin for another week anyway. So you've got time to make up your mind." He pushed back his chair and stood up. "Let me know just as soon as you decide."

That night, after the rest of the family had gone to bed, Ella sat in the kitchen with Mama and Papa, talking it over.

"You've got to think about this very carefully," Papa was saying. "Make sure it's what you want so you won't have

65

any regrets afterward." He paused. "You realize, Ella, this will change your whole life."

"I know, Papa. That's what scares me." She bit her lips and lapsed into troubled silence.

"You don't have to make up your mind this minute," Mama said.

Ella gripped her hands together. "I don't know what to do. If I give this up, I'll never again get such a chance. It's what I've dreamed about all my life," she cried out. "When I think about being on a stage singing before an audience, I could burst with happiness. But," her voice quavered, "a five-year contract! It's like signing my life away! Away from home and family. No time for anyone or anything. . . . And what about Jules?" His name trembled on her lips. A whole year away from New York! What would he say?

She reached out pleadingly. "Tell me what I should do."

Papa shook his head. "No Ella, in this case you've got to make up your own mind. You're not a child anymore." He stood up and paced restlessly back and forth. "It's your life and you'll have to live it, not us. Take your time. Don't rush. Think it over in your mind." His voice softened. "You know that whatever you decide, we'll stand by you and help all we can."

For a little while nothing more was said. Then Papa spoke again. "Before we do anything definite, I think we ought to have somebody who knows about such things look over the contract. After all, what do we know about show business and such things?"

"How about your cousins, the Timbergs?" suggested Mama. "They've been in vaudeville for years."

"You mean Herman Timberg?" Ella exclaimed. "Why

he's a headliner! He's even appeared at the Palace Theatre on Broadway. How is it you've never mentioned they were our relatives?"

Papa shrugged. "Somehow we've never had much to do with them. Their lives have been so different from ours. I don't know. We just never kept in touch. Actually Herman is a first cousin to me. I'll call up tomorrow and ask his advice."

And that's the way it was left.

The next night Papa came home all in a dither. "Luckily the Timberg family was in town. When I showed Herman the contract and he saw Mr. Woods's name on it, did he get excited. He said show people wait years for a chance to even get to see this man! He said Ella must really be something for him to take such an interest. When I began bringing up all sorts of objections, and how you couldn't make up your mind, he got very annoyed with me. What kind of nonsense was I talking? he said. And that I ought to thank God that Mr. Woods was giving Ella such a chance. His last words to me were 'It's a lucky break. Sign by all means!' "

8

Decision

Outwardly the rest of the momentous week flowed along as usual. Ella's relationship with the family, her singing lessons, her job seemed untouched. But underneath her composed manner, the need for coming to a decision kept gnawing away.

At home there was no further discussion about the contract. Ella was grateful for that. She sensed that Mama and Papa must have cautioned the sisters not to make mention of it. Only Charlotte, at dinner one night, said as if she were thinking out loud, "You know, Ella has a somewhere-else look on her face."

By Saturday Ella had made up her mind. She would sign the contract.

That night, she and Jules strolled to their favorite bench in the park. The air was touched with the fragrance of early spring. The night tiptoed around them, the dark trees like fingers raised for silence. Afraid of breaking the feeling of oneness between them, Ella shrank from bringing up the subject. But finally she could not stifle the words; they came tumbling out.

Jules listened, saying not a word. When she had finished, his head was lowered, his hands dug deep in his pockets. He seemed enveloped in a blanket of gloom. She wanted to reach out to touch him, but couldn't. All she could do was sit by numbly and wait.

He cleared his throat, as if it hurt him to talk. But when he spoke, his voice was calm, almost gentle. "Ella, I can't—I have no right to ask you not to do this. I have no right to impose *my* wishes—*my* hopes and dreams—on you." He laughed a bit ruefully. "If I did, some fine day, years from now, when I'm old and bald and fat, and we'd be sitting together, you'd look at me and think, And this is what I gave up a career for? I couldn't stand that. Besides, what have I got to offer you instead? Nothing. Just me.

"I'll have to work very hard this fall, what with a job and school at night. Not that I mind. No matter how tough the going will be. Because I realize it'll be working toward a future. Kind of selfish of me to imagine that *my* future, *my* career would be sufficient so that it would become yours too—*our* future. I keep forgetting that times are changing. Women are beginning to want to do more—to be more. Only"—he hesitated—"if you really loved me," his voice cracked, the pain now plainly visible in his face, "I don't think you'd even consider this contract. I'd figured that you'd want to help me, to encourage me, so I wouldn't have to go it all alone. It never occurred to me that you'd want to be off somewhere in Kalamazoo or someplace, pursuing a career of your own."

That's the male for you, Ella found herself thinking, resenting a woman's wanting a career outside of housewife and mother. It *was* selfish, as Jules himself had said.

Jules caught hold of her hand. "I'm sorry, Ella. I shouldn't have said that. It was unfair. Perhaps people like you, with great talent, should not be held back by marriage at all."

69

Again he retreated into stillness and she was left feeling shut out and alone.

She waited quietly until he said, "Maybe you should have this year, Ella. Maybe it will give you a chance to get this whole stage business out of your system." He took a deep breath. "Oh Ella, I'll miss you. The waiting—it'll be terrible. But I want you to know, I'll be here when you get back."

Tears trembled, hot and unbidden, beneath her eyelids. "I'll miss you too, Jules."

She knew that from now till the day of her departure from New York, her decision would lurk like a shadow between them.

Slowly they returned to Ella's house. At the doorway, they clung together for a long time, then silently parted.

Dismal and empty, Ella dragged herself up the stairs.

The light was still on in the kitchen. As she opened the door, the smell of fresh coffee tickled her nostrils. Comfortably gathered around the kitchen table were Mama, Papa, and Tanta.

"So—here's Ella," Tanta greeted her. "Just in time to join our coffee klatch. It's apple strudel this time. I baked it especially when I knew I was coming. It has a taste, whether you like it or not."

"How is it you're all up so late?" Ella asked.

"What do you think?" Papa replied. "Waiting for Henny. She and her boyfriends, they never know what time it is."

"Ella, I heard some wonderful news," Tanta ventured. "You're going on the stage! Oh my! What is it? An opera, maybe?"

"No, it's not an opera. It's a show," Ella replied shortly.

"Hmm. Lena and Hyman took me to a show once. They had acts with dogs and monkeys."

Everyone laughed. Even Ella managed a smile. "Oh Tanta."

"All right, all right. So there's no dogs with monkeys. So what kind of a thing is it?"

"It's an act with nine girls and one man. It's called 'Nine Crazy Kids.' "

" 'Nine crazy kids'? It sounds meshuga [crazy] to me. For that you needed all those singing lessons?"

Ella winced. "I'll be singing. It's just a beginning. After all, I have to get some experience. It's just as my cousin Herman told Papa—if I only learn to walk across a stage properly, I will have learned a lot."

"I never heard of such a thing! What's the matter, you don't know how to walk?" Tanta asked. "What are you, a baby all of a sudden? You walk, like everybody, with the feet."

Ella's spirits began to lift a bit. Right now, Tanta is a godsend, she reflected. Even the strudel was tasting better with every bite.

"So what do you intend?" persisted Tanta. "Are you going to walk or no?"

Ella contemplated the last morsel of strudel on her plate. "Yes," she said. "Yes, I am."

"Then it's settled!" Papa cried. "You're going to sign the contract!"

Ella nodded. She could feel Mama's searching gaze on her.

"You're sure?"

"Yes, Mama." Ella's voice was firm. "I'm sure."

71

"I wonder, is this a life for a nice Jewish girl?" Tanta asked.

"Nowadays there are plenty of nice Jewish girls on the stage," observed Mama.

"If they asked me," Tanta continued, "I wouldn't do it for a million dollars."

"First of all, Tanta, nobody is asking you," Papa declared. "Besides, Ella has to make her own choice."

"Choice-schmoice! She's still just a child."

"A person can't stay under her parents' roof forever," Ella retorted. "A girl leaves home when she gets married, doesn't she?"

"That's different!" scoffed Tanta. "When you get married, your husband takes over. Marriage and stage, they don't mix. It's one or the other. You wanna give up Jules?"

"I don't have to give him up. He's willing to wait."

"You think so, huh? Well, from what I see, there's plenty of other fish in the ocean, and with you away, some girl will snap him up just like that!" Tanta snapped her fingers. "Well, I'll never learn to keep my mouth from talking. You should excuse me for speaking out my mind. But you know I love Ella like she was my own child."

Mama put up her hand. "It's all right, Tanta."

She turned to Ella. "Tanta has expressed her feelings. Now let me tell you how I feel. I didn't say anything before. But now that you've made your choice, I can tell you."

"Tell me what?"

"Listen and you will understand. When I was a child," Mama began, "I sang too."

"Yes, I know."

"I know that story," Tanta interrupted. "Remember I was there."

Papa chuckled. "I know it too, even if I wasn't there."

"Please, the both of you, let me tell it to Ella," Mama pleaded. "So she'll appreciate it—and maybe you will too."

Tanta waved her on. "Go ahead and tell. Don't mind me."

"Many people praised my singing," Mama continued. "Everyone said I had an unusually fine voice and I was always asked to sing—in school, at parties and weddings.

"Of course, those were different days," she went on wistfully. "A career in the old country as a singer was a fantasy. At least that's what people like my parents believed. But my brother, the eldest in the family, he was different. He was sure that somehow, there was a great future in store for me.

"One day—one wonderful day—I must have been about ten years old, my brother took me to a voice teacher. And I sang for him." A poignant smile played around Mama's mouth. "He said that my voice held great promise but that I was still too young for training. He told my brother to bring me back when I was fourteen and he would be more than happy to take me on as one of his pupils.

"You can imagine how thrilled I was." She sighed; it came from deep inside her. "My brother was resolved to pay for the lessons. My parents couldn't. But by the time I was fourteen, my brother was already in the army." She halted, her hands opening in a gesture of futility. "Then he died . . . my one hope. . . . Pneumonia, they said. . . . And that was the end of my singing career.

"It is something you never forget for a whole lifetime.

That is why Papa and I always managed to squeeze out a little extra for your piano and singing lessons."

She swept a hand across her face as if to wipe away the sadness of the memory, but in the next moment, looking straight at Papa, her face suddenly seemed transformed. It was shining with pride. "But my childhood dream did not die, after all. It is alive! It lives on through Ella!"

"So now you want Ella should make up for what you lost?" Tanta murmured.

Mama flushed. "Oh no! It's not like that at all. Why do you think I've never told Ella this before? I didn't want her to be influenced by what had happened in my life. Ella must do whatever she believes is best for her—and for her only."

Tanta's chin thrust forward, her arms akimbo. "You're sorry, maybe?" she challenged Mama. "You think you missed something? You think maybe you would have had a better life on the stage?"

"Of course not!" Mama returned quickly. "Only sometimes, in a fleeting moment, I catch myself thinking—what would it have been like?"

Smiling apologetically at Papa, she reached for his hands and cradled them in her own. "For myself, I would not change for anything! We've had our full share of hard times and troubles, but I'm nonetheless deeply content. I have found my great satisfaction—more than that—my greatest joy in sharing my life with Papa and in raising a fine family."

She turned to Ella. "But that was right for me, Ella. For your life, only you can answer."

"Oh Mama!" Ella threw her arms around her. "Hold fast to that dream! I won't let you down, I promise!"

"No, Ella, no promises. That would be a big mistake. Just do what will make you happy."

"And if you'll be happy and Mama will be happy, and Tanta will be happy, then I'll be happy, too. And the entire family will be like a bunch of happy hooligans," Papa cried, laughing all over himself.

9

Prancing Pony

Ella had taken it for granted that rehearsals would be held in a theatre. To her surprise, the address given turned out to be a room in a shabby old building somewhere on Sixth Avenue. It was a barnlike place with paint peeling from the walls and grimy windows looking out on an alley. A few chairs, a coat rack, and a forlorn-looking piano scarred by countless cigarette butts completed the picture.

The company was already assembled. Ella counted eight girls and one man besides Mr. Trent and the piano player. They were standing around chatting with an air of easy camaraderie.

Mr. Trent caught sight of her. "Hiya," he greeted and came forward to help her off with her cape.

A blur of introductions followed—Sally, La Verne, Marian, the fellow named Jack. But one thing did register. The girls were all young and their faces were heavily made up. As for that Jack, was he supposed to be the juvenile lead? He must be forty at least! And all that patent leather grease on his hair! Ugh!

"Okay now, girls," Mr. Trent called out, "let's get started." He pulled a chair into the center of the room and sat down, the troupe gathering around him.

"First, we'll go over the tunes. Hand out the music sheets, somebody." He snapped his fingers. "Let's go, Harry," and the pianist plunged into the first song.

The melodies were lively and simple enough for everyone to follow—but what voices! Ella couldn't help thinking Professor Calvano would have grabbed his hat and made a hasty exit.

Over and over they sang, till everyone was familiar with the lyrics.

"All right, kids, you can take a break now," Mr. Trent announced. "Not you, Miss Ella. You've got a solo to learn. And there's a duet with Jack, too."

Immediately Ella could sense some lifting of eyebrows, an exchange of glances.

"Miss Ella's solo, Harry," Mr. Trent directed. "Take it from the top."

Ella listened intently to the introduction, then followed the music and words on her song sheet. What a silly tune, she thought. Nevertheless, she sang it with as much feeling as she could. When she'd finished, Mr. Trent was smiling, all friendly. "That's good. A little more swing, maybe. But that'll come as we work on it. Now let's try the duet."

Jack's was not much of a voice, Ella decided, but she had to admit he did know how to put over a song in a slambang style.

"When both of you have got it down pat," Mr. Trent said, "we'll put in the dance steps. Jack, that routine we worked out, you'll teach it to Miss Ella."

"Be my pleasure, baby," Jack whispered in her ear, sliding his arm around her. Ella stiffened.

"Now let's see." Mr. Trent turned to the girls. "You,

77

Irene," pointing to a pert redhead with a turned-up nose, "you'll be Miss Ella's understudy. We'll rehearse you in the song next time. Harry, give her a song sheet."

Did Ella imagine it or did Irene's nose tilt a bit higher? I guess she doesn't like the idea of playing understudy to a mere beginner like me.

"Okay now, girls! Line up for the dance. Snap into it! Size places. Miss Ella, you're the smallest. You're first."

Ella was in a panic. She wanted to cry out "I'm not a dancer!" but Mr. Trent was already demonstrating the first step. "You come on in a pony prance with your knees up high. Like this."

Thank heavens, the step looks easy enough, Ella thought, relieved.

But the dancing was far from satisfying to Mr. Trent. "Go on back—all of you—and try it again," he shouted.

Over and over the girls pranced till Ella found herself gasping for breath.

"Take ten," Mr. Trent finally yelled.

Now what does that mean? Ella wondered. When she saw the group dispersing around the room and Mr. Trent relax against the side of the piano, she understood it meant a ten-minute rest. Gratefully she sank into a chair.

All too soon, the ten minutes were up. Rehearsal of the dance routine resumed. It seemed easy enough for the others, but Ella found the steps a crazy patch quilt of legs. I'll never get it! Which foot? Right? Left? Kicks, endless circles. My legs are dropping off.

"Step and kick and circle in the air!" Mr. Trent barked out anew.

The line of legs bobbed up and down like a jumping centipede. Ella, in desperation, kicked too hard. Her right

78

leg shot up and, unbalanced, she started teetering backward. Immediately, one after the other, the girls fell back like a row of falling dominoes.

By a stroke of good luck, Jack, seated on a chair at the line's end, was able to put out his hands just in time. He caught the last dancer as she promptly collapsed in his lap. The pianist stopped playing and looked inquiringly at Mr. Trent as the group disentangled itself amid a grumble of taunting remarks.

Ella burst into tears. "I'm sorry. I'm very sorry," she kept reiterating.

But to everyone's amazement, Mr. Trent was all smiles. "Great!" he cried.

Ella's mouth dropped open in the midst of a sob. She smiled at Mr. Trent uncertainly.

"Miss Ella, you've given me a great idea!" Mr. Trent went on. "We can use that whole setup in the finale for the dance. By golly, it looks just like a row of falling ninepins!"

The girls all looked at one another. "But Mr. Trent," one of them ventured, "a stunt like that will be hard to come out of."

"So we'll practice it, till we get it right. It's sensational! It's way too good to lose. Well. That's all for today. We'll continue working on it tomorrow. 10 A.M. sharp!"

Ella was silent and subdued as Mr. Trent escorted her to the subway station. "Don't worry so much, Miss Ella," he said. "See what you came up with today? Everything will be all right. Keep smiling." He threw her a quizzical glance, tipped his hat, and walked on.

His heartening words helped somewhat. But for the greater part of her ride homeward, Ella sat slumped in her seat, exhausted in body and spirit. How am I ever going to go through with this? It's all so different from what I imagined.

At least I have a solo. Only how I wish it were a different kind of song. Sure vaudeville's not opera. But there are so many lovely songs people would enjoy hearing. Yet it does give me a chance to be noticed. Maybe some big producer or director will see me. . . .

When you're a star on Broadway, you'll have your choice of songs to sing. Right now don't complain. Be grateful for small favors. Like that crazy thing that happened during the dancing today. I started out crying and ended up laughing. If it hadn't turned out that way, I don't know how I could have gone on.

At home she managed to parry the family's innumerable pryings with trumped-up enthusiasm. "Everything's fine. Of course it's hard work, especially the dancing part. Imagine me dancing! Mr. Trent's a real stickler for perfection. He makes you go over every step a hundred times! Please everyone, I'm awfully tired."

The daily rehearsals went on. Ella was given over completely to her work. She toiled away all the more single-mindedly because she felt so isolated. The other girls went out together, exchanged confidences, even borrowed money from one another. But somehow she was never included. And Mr. Trent's preferential treatment of her didn't help any either. It only served to fan the resentment some of them must have felt. Occasionally she'd overhear a remark like "Get a load of that *Miss* Ella. The prima donna!" and she'd wish she could shrink away into nothingness.

Toward the end of the week, Mr. Trent started to work

on the final routine. A tricky little step kept eluding her.

"Left foot, kid. Cross it over right," a voice close by whispered.

It was Sally—Sally, the peroxide blonde with the baby blue eyes. "Take it easy, kid. You're getting yourself tied up in knots over nothing." Ella flashed her a grateful smile.

When Mr. Trent called a break, Sally pulled her aside. "C'mere, kid. Lemme show you."

Patiently, she broke the step down and it became suddenly clear. Ella had finally made herself a friend.

But with each passing day, Ella found herself growing more and more dispirited. "I suppose the rehearsing is the hardest part," she remarked to Sally. "Once you're actually performing, it's fun, isn't it?"

"Are you kiddin'?" Sally returned. "With four shows a day! And hangin' around in between waiting to go on? It ain't too much fun!" She shrugged her shoulders. "But you get used to it."

"Get used to it!" Ella exclaimed. "When I think of having to work with Jack for a whole year . . ." She shuddered.

"Don't be so fussy, kid. He's not so bad."

"Putting his arm around me every chance he gets! Even pinching me!" Ella cried, her annoyance spilling out.

Sally laughed good-naturedly. "Relax, kid. He's just a big dope. He doesn't mean any harm, really."

Ella sighed. "You're a lot more tolerant than I am."

"Live and let live I say," Sally replied matter-of-factly.

*   *   *

By the following week, rehearsals had stepped up intensively. Mr. Trent's cheery manner was evaporating. "What the devil do you think you're doing?" he would yell at the cast. "Can't you pick up your feet, you lummoxes? Don't stand there gaping at me like half-wits! Go back and take the entrance again!"

Sullenly the girls muttered under their breath. One needs real grit to stand up to this, Ella fumed, frequently close to tears herself. But if they can bear it, so can I.

"You know," she later remarked to Jules, "when we finally win a grudging grunt of approval from Mr. Trent, it's like winning a victory."

"A victory over what?" Jules asked with a touch of sarcasm.

"A victory over myself!" she shot back.

"So you've learned to kick up your feet in time to music. Is that so important?" Jules went on. "And what has that to do with your singing?"

"When you take on a job, you work at it till you can do it well," Ella replied hotly. "Or at least you keep trying. Besides, knowing something about dancing won't do my career any harm."

"I suppose not," Jules admitted. "Forget it. Let's not argue over it."

They were pulling apart. Ella could feel it and it made her miserable. She yearned to be with Jules, but often rehearsals were late, cutting into the time they'd planned to spend together. When they were together, she was too fatigued to want to do anything or go anywhere. They'd just sit around in the parlor or downstairs. She would ask Jules about his job, but all the while he'd be talking, her mind would be occupied with problems concerning the show. Jules would notice her dwindling attention, and after a few minutes, he'd lapse into silence.

It's just a couple of weeks and already we're drifting away from each other. What's going to happen in a year? Ella asked herself desolately.

10

Follow the Leader

"Whee!" yelled red-haired Pat. He grabbed hold of the lamp post, swinging himself up and around in a flying circle. Jumping clear, he landed on both feet, waving on the line of six boys behind him.

"C'mon, you guys!"

One after the other they followed suit.

Charlie sat on the curb watching longingly. Wish I could play with them. But they're way bigger and older than me.

"Hey, kid, wanna join?" Pat called out.

Charlie sprang up. "Uh-huh!"

Pat grinned. "You'll have to keep up."

"Okay!" Charlie cried.

Next moment, he too was swinging around the pole. By the time he was back on the pavement, Pat had led his followers down the length of the block and around the corner.

Charlie went dashing madly after, forgetting completely Mama's warning, "Stay close to the house!"

Now Pat bounded up the stoop of a tenement. Pausing briefly, knees bent, he spread-eagled his arms and jumped down to the sidewalk.

Jump! Jump! Jump! in quick succession, and then it

84

was Charlie's turn. It's easy, he decided. Galloping down the stairs in his own house, he had jumped like that lots of times.

Wham! He made it! On he flew after the others.

In, out, and round about in a snakelike dance, Pat wove his gang. Suddenly he spied an ash can. With the agility of a cat, he leapfrogged over. The followers too sailed safely across, though somewhat less gracefully.

Charlie took a deep breath. Pressing his hands firmly down on either side of the can, he hurled himself upward. Alas, he couldn't quite clear the top.

"Up you go, kid!" Someone grabbed him by the seat of his pants and hoisted him over. It was Pat!

Across the gutter the line streaked in a race to reach the other side before an oncoming streetcar. Clang, clang! Frantically the conductor slammed his heel down hard on the bell. But by then, the boys were safely across.

"We did it!" the youngsters crowed, panting and shivering a little at their flirtation with danger.

"C'mon!" Pat commanded. "Forward march, fellers!"

The street just ahead was all broken up. For days laborers had been working, repairing the gas mains. It was late afternoon and they had already gone. Across the wide opening of the excavation, some wooden planks had been laid. At either end, a red warning lantern glowed.

"There's only one way to get across this big hole," Pat announced. "Walking across the boards."

"Gee, they're pretty far apart," one boy said.

"That they are. And they're kinda narrow, too. Scared?"

"Who me? Nah!" the others boasted. Nonetheless, they watched nervously as Pat stepped on the first board. It swayed beneath his weight. Quickly he moved on to the next board, and the next, till finally he was on firm ground.

"What are you waiting for, fellers?" he scoffed.

Slowly, cautiously, the next boy in line began the hazardous journey. One after the other the rest of the gang followed, till at last all save Charlie were on the other side.

Charlie stood eyeing the first board. The other side was so far away. Six boards away! The spaces between them seemed much further apart now that he was close to them. Below, the pit gaped, deep, dark, and forbidding. If he should make just one false step!

"Hey, kid, better skip this one," advised Pat.

Charlie's head came up. "I can do it!" he shouted.

He stretched one leg a giant step forward. There! He was safe on the first board! Slowly he managed the next. See, I can do it, he egged himself on. But the others were growing impatient at his snail's pace.

"Aw, come on!" they cried. "You're holding up the game!"

Charlie pushed himself to go faster. There was just one more board to conquer.

But the gap looked too wide. He glanced back. It was too far away to go back. He had to go on! But he'd have to jump if he was ever going to make it. There was no other way.

Charlie clenched his fists; his body grew taut, and he jumped! . . . There was nothing there but empty space. . . . He was falling, his small body plummeting downward! With a thud, his head struck a huge pipe.

Charlie lay crumpled at the bottom of the pit. He knew no more. . . .

Ella sat beside Mama and Papa in the hospital waiting room. How long had they been there? It seemed an eternity since Charlie had been admitted. She stole a glance at Mama. How pale she was! Her eyes appeared to have sunk deep in their sockets. For once, her never idle hands lay inert in her lap.

And Papa? Where were the laugh lines in his face now? Lips tight with anguish, his gaze was riveted on the door leading to the hospital corridor.

Ella longed to enfold them both in her arms—to say something that might help, but her tongue clove to the roof of her mouth.

What was taking so long? Not knowing was so terrifying.

Footsteps echoed down the length of the corridor. They seemed headed their way. Yes, finally, it was the doctor.

"The boy is still unconscious. There is concussion. We do not yet know the extent of damage." He spread his hands in a gesture of helplessness. "There's little more we can do right now."

"Could we see him?" Papa asked.

"Not just yet." The doctor put a hand on Papa's arm. "We're doing everything possible." It was both a promise and a hope.

Papa nodded. "He's our only son," he said huskily.

Trouble—how quickly it can strike, Ella reflected as the three walked out into the night. Just a few short hours ago, everything at home had been serene. And now this sudden calamity! She choked back her tears. Thank heaven the show has not gone on the road yet. Right now I must be with the family.

Days and nights of anxiety held each other by the tail.

There seemed no change in Charlie's condition. The girls tiptoed around the house, fearful of shattering the silence into which Mama and Papa had retreated. Like them, they too were holding at bay a constant dread of what might happen.

At rehearsals, Mr. Trent was driving his performers. "Snap it up! Keep it gay!"

How can I go skipping about and singing at such a time? Ella thought. I guess this is what they mean when they say "The show must go on!" I must learn to make myself perform in spite of anything.

Late one evening Mama and Papa and Ella returned from the hospital. As the others gathered round, Mama informed them, "They've moved Charlie into the isolation building."

"Does that mean Charlie's going to die?" Gertie whimpered.

Henny shook her little sister. "Don't say that! Don't even think it!"

"No Gertie," Mama assured her, "it's just that Charlie was disturbing the other patients in the room."

At least that's what the nurse had said, Ella told herself. In her mind's eye she saw again the grim, forbidding building set apart from the rest of the hospital where Charlie now lay. Had the doctor despaired of Charlie? Was this his way of preparing us for the dreaded possibility? Please God, she prayed silently, let it not be!

Henny broke into her thoughts. "Mama, maybe they could put Charlie in a private room."

Papa shook his head. "We couldn't afford that. Besides, the nurse says it wouldn't make any difference. Charlie doesn't know where he is. He just keeps calling out and mumbling things that make no sense."

"Sometimes he catches on to something you say and he repeats it over and over," Mama added. "It's awful!" She put her hands to her ears as if to shut out the sound.

There was nothing else anyone could say. An all-encompassing gloom, like some thick vapor, was closing in on them with each tick of the clock. Mama regarded the sad faces around her. Then quietly she said, "It's getting late. Time you children got to sleep."

The girls all went off to bed, save Ella, who followed Mama and Papa into the kitchen.

"Shall I make some coffee, Mama?" Ella asked.

Mama nodded.

"Uncle Hyman came to see me again today," Papa remarked. "He keeps begging me to speak to the rabbi about changing Charlie's name."

"Changing Charlie's name?" repeated Ella.

"Yes. It's an old, old Jewish ritual that goes back hundreds of years. It is done at a time like this, when a person is very sick."

"I've heard something about it somewhere, Papa. But why is it done? What's its purpose?"

"I have a book which explains better than I can."

Papa looked questioningly at Mama. "Will it upset you if I read to Ella about it?"

Mama shook her head. So Papa went to his room and came back with an old volume in his hand. He rifled through the yellowed pages. "Here it is. It's written in Hebrew but I'll translate it for you." Adjusting his glasses, he began to read.

" 'It is believed that when the Angel of Death comes for a person, he calls him by name. To confuse the Angel, the dying one is given a new name. When they do this, the

89

loved ones are saying, *Go away, Angel of Death. The one lying here is not the one you seek. He is someone else bearing a different name. Whatever fate you may have in store for that other one, you cannot apply to this one.*

" 'Sometimes the new name is chosen by opening a Bible at random and picking out a name which may appear on that page. But more often, one is chosen which has a meaning. For example, Haim or Haya, which means life—or Hezekiah, meaning May God give strength—or Raphael, meaning May God heal. This new name is added to the sick one's name.

" 'The change is then discussed with the rabbi, who announces it in the synagogue. A special prayer is recited, part of which reads, *Just as his name has been changed, so may the evil decree passed on him be changed—from justice to mercy—from sickness to complete recovery.*' "

"The whole thing sounds so strange, Papa. It's like something out of the Middle Ages."

"It is a ceremony that still goes on, Ella. Of course we know that our fate lies in the hands of the Almighty—not in ours. But it is a last desperate hope—like a prayer we offer up to God. Surely, Ella, prayer can never hurt, can it?"

A week went by and then came joyous news! Charlie had been transferred back to the ward.

"The doctor says Charlie's going to be all right," Ella cried.

"You mean Charles-Irving. Remember? He has a new name," reminded Sarah.

"Oh Papa! Oh Mama! Isn't it wonderful?" the other children joined in.

"Yes," agreed Papa. "It's a miracle. A miracle from God!" His eyes held the suspicion of tears.

Charlotte sidled up to Papa and took his hand. "Papa, I guess the Angel of Death really got fooled, didn't he?"

"Yes, my child." Papa smiled. "It happened. It really happened."

Long after the others had finally gone to bed, Ella sat in the kitchen talking things over with Mama.

"Ella," Mama said after a pause in the conversation, "there's something I want to tell you."

"What is it, Mama?" Ella asked, instantly alarmed.

"Don't worry. It's a different kind of news this time." She hesitated. "I had wanted to tell you sooner, but with this terrible thing hanging over us—" She waited a moment, then said quickly, "Ella, I'm going to have another child."

"Mama! Oh what a surprise! I just can't believe it!"

"I wasn't sure how you'd take the news." Mama looked away. She seemed to be talking to the wall. "Here Ella is, a grown woman, practically engaged to be married, and her mother's going to have a baby! Will she be embarrassed?"

"Embarrassed! Oh Mama! I'll be so happy and proud!"

Mama blew a sigh and turned back to face Ella. "Well, my eldest, I'm very much relieved. Papa and I, we knew it meant another mouth to feed, and that we were not young anymore. But when Charlie was so sick, when we were afraid we might lose him, how very precious each child seemed to us then. I wondered all along, was this God's way of granting me another child? If God in his infinite wisdom saw fit to take our son away from us, was he perhaps giving us another son in his stead?"

"There hasn't been a baby around the house for such a

long time, Mama, everyone will be delighted. How could you even dream we wouldn't want it? But Mama, I just thought of something. Suppose it's another girl?"

"Would we love her any the less for being a girl?"

11

Onstage

"Okay everyone, gather around," Mr. Trent announced after a particularly grueling workout. Snapping his fingers for attention, he suddenly went into a series of tricky dance steps winding up with a high kick way over his head.

"This," he stretched his arms out dramatically, "is our final rehearsal!"

General merriment and applause burst forth from the company.

Sally grinned at Ella's astonishment. "He used to be quite a hoofer way back when," she whispered.

When the hubbub had quieted down, Mr. Trent continued. "And now I've got some good news. We've already got enough bookings around New York and New Jersey to keep us working in this area all summer. So it looks like we won't be heading elsewhere till sometime after Labor Day."

Ella's heart skipped a beat. This was it. No turning back now. But she was glad they weren't leaving just yet. She'd be able to be with Jules.

At suppertime, Ella spilled the exciting news to the family. "Our first performance will be given at the DeKalb Theatre in Brooklyn."

"Isn't it lucky!" Sarah exclaimed. "We'll be able to come and see your act."

"I just can't wait to find out what it's all about," Henny cried. "You've never let any of us come down to watch even one rehearsal. You've kept the whole thing such a mystery, we're all dying of curiosity."

Ella tried to make light of the whole thing. "Oh, don't make such a fuss. After all, it's just a vaudeville skit."

"But I like vaudeville," Henny declared. "Seeing real people on a stage with an orchestra. When the acts are over and the movie comes on, everything seems so flat by comparison."

"But it's such a long ride out to Brooklyn. Why should you bother?" Even as she said this, Ella realized she was trying to discourage them from coming, but she wasn't quite sure why.

"A bother!" Papa cried. "To see our daughter make her first appearance on a professional stage!"

"We gotta go too," Gertie and Charlotte insisted.

"Don't worry, Ella," Mama assured her, "we won't come for the very first show. We'll give you a chance to get used to it."

Mama figures I'm just nervous about performing. I wonder what she'll think when she sees me romping around in a kid's dress singing silly songs? Oh, what does it matter? They're going to come anyway. If they're disappointed . . . well . . .

"You know what," Mama suggested, "I think it would be nice for Bill and Grace, and her parents to come along too."

"And I'll invite a couple of my friends," Henny added.

"Sure! Why not?" Ella yelled, suddenly exasperated. "Invite the whole neighborhood."

Dress rehearsal had been called for 9 A.M. But much before that Ella was already pacing back and forth inside the deserted theatre entrance. She kept reading and re-reading the new attractions for the week posted in the glass cases on either side of the lobby. Each time her eyes would stop at the number-four spot announcing the Nine Crazy Kids to make sure that it was really there. How she had dreamed of just this! Someday, maybe, her name would blaze in lights on the theatre marquee.

She looked at her watch. It was time to get backstage.

Just inside the stage door, a little old man was sitting on a chair, head buried in a newspaper. Glancing up he motioned with his thumb. "Upstairs."

He accepts me. I belong, Ella exulted as she threaded her way up the narrow iron stairs. A babble of voices and laughter issuing through a door was direction enough. She went in.

"Over here, Ella!" Sally's voice could be heard above the din. "I saved you a spot." She shoved over her belongings to make room.

Ella looked around. One tiny window, several bare electric bulbs hanging from the ceiling. Along one wall, a wide shelf like a counter in a shop, a large tarnished mirror above it with a glaring light on either side. It was piled high with an assortment of makeup kits. Clothes and costumes were draped helter-skelter over chairs or hung from hooks on the smudged gray walls.

"*Spot* is right," Ella observed. "Do we all have to squeeze into one dressing room?"

"Listen to her." Irene's voice had an edge of malice. "What'd you expect? A dressing room all for yourself? With a star painted on the door, maybe?"

Ella flushed. "No, of course not. I just didn't know."

"This is luxury, kid!" Marian exclaimed with a toss of her pumpkin-colored dyed hair. "Wait till you get a load of some of the dumps out on the road. You'll be glad if you get as much as a curtain to dress behind." She burst into laughter. "Say, Irene, remember what happened to that George Stanley?"

Irene giggled. "I sure do. That was a scream."

"What's so funny?" the others demanded. "Let us in on it."

"Well," Irene began, "it happened in some hick town out west. I forget now just which. Anyway, there was this guy, George Stanley, a real spiffy dresser. Spats, cane, flower in his buttonhole—the works. He was always struttin' around, showin' off before us girls. He was sure convinced he was a lady killer.

"Well, there was no dressing room in that theatre. We had to dress behind a screen backstage. George was gettin' ready for the matinee show. He did a song-and-dance routine—and the screen toppled over. There, right in front of everybody, stood George in long flannel underwear! Red, no less! Boy, you shoulda seen the look on his face! That finished George for us girls. We could never think of him as a lady killer anymore."

"Well anyway, it's not so bad here," Sally remarked to Ella after the laughter had died down. "It's pretty clean, too. You should see some of the filthy holes they call dressing rooms. You freeze in the winter and melt away in the summer."

"You can say that again!" A pert-faced girl named Mary emerged from the crush at the mirror to grin goodnaturedly at Sally. "I remember once an act I was with got stuck up north in another small town. They had a regular blizzard. We were stayin' in some crummy hotel and the pipes froze. So there was no heat. Was it cold! Brr-rr! So six of us girls piled into one bed trying to keep warm. We were packed together like sardines. Nobody got a wink of sleep jabbering away and laughing all night. But we had such a good time we never even minded the cold. Then, just before dawn, the bed collapsed!"

Ella exchanged smiles with the others but she wondered whether she would really find that so funny.

With all the other acts on the bill battling for equal time and attention, final rehearsal was hectic. Down in the pit the musicians sat waiting, indifferent and bored, while the harried house manager tried to arrange things so as to satisfy everyone. When they did play, the conductor rushed them through the music, for the most part ignoring the demands of the exasperated performers. Somehow though, Ella noted, everyone managed to get through. Afterward they all dashed across the street to a lunchroom for a quick bite.

"Well, Sally, it seems we're already a big success," Ella commented wryly as she munched her sandwich. "We're appearing on the same bill with an animal act."

Sally chuckled. "Yeah. An' they'll probably get a bigger hand from the audience than we will. Audiences love it," she went on. "I guess from where they sit, it all looks so cute—the little dogs jumping through hoops an' prancin' around the stage, or cats or monkeys all dressed up. Believe me, if they could only see what it's like for those

97

poor dumb creatures backstage, they wouldn't think it was so cute."

She stared moodily into her cup of coffee. "Why am I feelin' so sorry for the animals? In vaudeville, actors lead a dog's life too. Always on the move. Never stayin' long enough to get to see the town or know the people. You leave for the railroad station the minute the curtain drops on the last show, an' get to the next town with hardly time to slap on your makeup and snap into your place onstage. Why, sometimes to make connections, a day could go by with you never gettin' near a bed at all. You just sleep sittin' up on the train. Livin' off sandwiches, or chocolate bars, or an apple or somethin'. Phew!" She shrugged disgustedly.

Ella's eyes searched Sally's face. She's strong. She can endure this kind of life. Can I? "Then why do you go on, Sally?" she asked.

"It's because I've got greasepaint in my veins, I guess. You go along hopin' someday maybe you'll get a break. Make the big time. You know—be on the stage at the Palace, say." She laughed scornfully. "Fat chance for a nothin' talent like me." Her finger jabbed at Ella. "Now if I had a voice like yours . . ." With a flick of the finger, she tossed away the impossible. "Actually, Ella, it don't much matter if I never get any further than this. I'm doin' pretty good. After all, I'm in the theatre, and that's for me. I'd rather be up there on that stage than doin' anythin' else in the whole world!"

More than anything else in the whole world, Ella repeated silently. The very words Mr. Woods had used when she'd first met him. That's the way I'm supposed to feel. But do I? Well, I am excited about the performance today.

98

I can hardly wait. Oh, for heaven's sake! Will I ever stop this seesawing back and forth? I've got a show to put on! Forget about everything else!

Back in the dressing room, Sally helped her with her makeup. I look like a doll, Ella decided as she stared at her reflection in the mirror.

"Ten minutes!" came the warning. There was a last smoothing of hair, a last tug at a costume, a last dab of powder on a painted face.

"Remember now, girls," Mr. Trent's hand went up for emphasis, "if you don't want the act to flop, you gotta grab hold of the audience the minute you step out on that stage. There's no time for a slow buildup. So snap into it! Fast and furious! And keep it like that till the finish. Get it?"

"Okay," the girls cried.

"Don't worry, Mr. Trent," Jack added, very self-assured. "We'll knock 'em dead."

As they waited in the wings, Ella felt herself trembling. Was it stage fright? Just then Sally's hand touched her shoulder. "Do like we rehearsed and you'll be swell!"

"Thanks," Ella whispered gratefully.

Onstage two comics were winding up their act to a smattering of applause. The curtain descended. On either side, a stagehand changed the placards in the racks announcing the new act. And then, the curtain was going up for them!

Their entrance music! Ella forced a smile to her lips, and with the precision born of much practice, led the line of prancing ponies out.

Suddenly, how marvelous it was! The lights—the scenery —the people out there. They had actually paid to see her.

Silly though the act might be, nothing mattered now except that she was performing.

The act was going well, she could sense it. Time now for her solo. As she began, Ella could feel an immediate response from the audience. All rustlings, all whisperings ceased. It was as if out there beyond the footlights, people were caught up completely by what she was telling them. The applause at the end was like a bouquet of their appreciation and made Ella glow with happiness and pride.

When the act was over, everybody was hilariously happy. "They liked it!" "We wowed them!" There were hugs and kisses, pats on the back, and impromptu jigs all along the hallway and into the dressing room.

"It went so fast!" Ella confided breathlessly to Sally. "It seemed to be over before we even got started." She shook her head. "To think of the weeks it took to rehearse."

"Hmm," Sally sniffed, "wait till you've done the act a couple of hundred times. It won't be short enough."

But for now, Ella would not let anything dampen her elation. "Yes, but at every performance the audience will be different. That should make it interesting—challenging."

Sally's lips twitched in a smile but she said nothing.

As the week progressed, the glow still clung. Ella did not seem to mind the long waits between shows—so much time on their hands yet never enough to get too far away from the theatre. To compensate there was the friendly exchange with members of the other acts, the fun of invading a nearby lunchroom with the troupe still in makeup and the stares of the other diners. Even the long ride home each night was not dull when shared with such a lively bunch of fellow actors.

Yet in the midst of the flow of impressions pouring in on her, the thought of Jules kept recurring like a beloved refrain. She had not heard from him all week. But tomorrow was Saturday. He was coming up to see the last show.

Her musings were interrupted by a surprise visitor in the dressing room. It was Mr. Woods and he was all smiles.

"I caught the act tonight," he said, pumping Ella's hand. "You were okay! Okay! You came across those footlights just like I figured!"

After he left, Ella tried hard to hold on to his words so full of promise even as the vision of Jules rose before her. Had Jules missed her? Had he been lonesome for her? Could he have gone out with someone else? A mothwing of jealousy brushed against her. Oh no! He couldn't! He wouldn't!

All through the Saturday-night show, Ella kept wishing she could pierce the curtain of darkness beyond the footlights. Jules was out there! What was he thinking about all this? Oh, I just can't wait to see him!

The moment the curtain came down, she dashed up the stairs, removed her makeup, and hastily redressed. She was out the stage door before anyone else.

There he was, coming toward her. Her heart gave a little skip. How handsome he was! So clean-cut, his deep blue eyes bright now with the gladness of seeing her. Catching hold of her in his strong arms, he gazed down at her face as if he could never be done with looking. She laughed a little, averting her head, breathless with ardor and embarrassment.

With evident pride, yet with a touch of shyness, she introduced him to the company as they emerged through the door. The girls swarmed about him like a flock of bees. "You're kinda cute. You haven't got a brother by any chance?" "Say, kid, where'd you pick this one up?"

Somewhat abashed by their good-natured jibing, Jules's face reddened. And then Jack came by.

"Hiya, son!" he said, giving Jules a resounding slap on the back. "Ouch!" He grimaced comically, shaking his fingers. "This boy's got muscles. My hand's busted!"

Ella could see Jules stiffen. "It's getting late," she said quickly. "We'd better be going."

"So long, Jules." "Come see us again!" Smiles, a wave of the hand, and a broad wink from Sally. Jules tipped his hat to the girls, nodded to Jack, and off they went.

As they reached the corner, Jules pursed his lips and exhaled slowly. Sensing his unspoken criticism, Ella bridled with a strange rush of loyalty. I'm like a mother, she thought in silent vexation—a mother who can say anything she likes about her child's shortcomings. But just let anyone else point them out . . .

"I know you think they're kind of crude, Jules. So they are. But you've got to understand all kinds of people and accept them for what they are. Besides, I've found out that underneath their rough speech and flashy appearance, they're really nice. They're warmhearted and generous. Good sports, too. And certainly hardworking."

Jules looked at her. "You needn't apologize for them. I'm no snob."

"I wasn't apologizing," she returned. "Just explaining." She broke off abruptly, suddenly feeling very tired. She had so looked forward to this night. Now see how, right at the start, they were pulling apart again. She tried to smile. "I must admit I don't care too much for that Jack."

102

"That makes two of us," Jules affirmed with conviction.

He hasn't mentioned one word about my performance, Ella fretted. Well, she wouldn't ask him. And then in the next moment, she found herself saying, "Well? How did I do?"

"You were very good."

"But?"

"It's not exactly like singing in the Temple choir." He stared straight ahead. "Last year when I was in the army and the High Holy Days came around, I kept remembering how we both used to sing together in the Temple. And I'd think—well, maybe next year. I guess . . ." His voice sounded despondent. ". . . it won't be this year either."

Ella tried to change the conversation. "How's your job?" she ventured.

"Oh, all right. The work's pretty routine but the place is pleasant enough."

"I suppose you can't wait till fall when you'll be back at school."

He nodded. "I'm anxious to get going. It'll be good for me. Keep my mind off . . ." He turned his head away and scanned the dark shapes of the brownstone buildings along the street.

It's no use, Ella realized unhappily. No matter what we talk about, we always come back to the same thing.

On the long subway ride home, they tried to cover the gulf between themselves with small talk. From the station to Ella's house they walked, arms linked, but their thoughts were separate and lonely. It's been so hopeless—the whole evening, Ella brooded. Her inward lament sounded louder in her ears than the echo of their footsteps on the pavement.

103

They were at her door. She raised her face to his. Her voice low, she asked, "Will I see you tomorrow?"

"You want me to?"

"Yes."

Their eyes met. He opened his arms and she went into them. For the moment, the emptiness was gone. He kissed her softly on the lips. "Good-bye, till tomorrow."

Ella turned swiftly so that he would not see her tears.

12

Seesaw

"You're stuck on that Jules, aren't you?" Sally remarked as they were getting ready for the act.

"Uh-huh."

"Well, he's certainly nuts about you. It's written all over him." Sally waved her powder puff at Ella. "Listen, kid, take my advice and grab him. His kind doesn't come our way often, believe me."

"You ever think about getting married, Sally?"

"What girl doesn't?"

"But suppose you did get married, would you go on with your career?"

Sally looked thoughtfully into the mirror as she outlined her eyes with black pencil. "I don't know. If the man I married was in the theatre, I guess I would. But then, if we had kids—" she shook her head. "It sure would complicate things. I've seen lots of those marriages. Mothers parking their babies in dresser drawers in hotels and in baskets in the dressing rooms. The poor babies constantly being dragged around from town to town. Then when they're ready for school, stickin' 'em away somewhere with relatives while you have to go traipsin' around the country. Never gettin' a chance to be with them." She spread out her arms. "Now I ask you, what kinda life is that for a family?"

Ella twisted uneasily. "But suppose you met someone who wanted to marry you that wasn't in show business?"

"So if I liked him enough, I'd marry him." Her husky voice grew almost wistful. "Yeah. It might be kinda nice havin' a home of my own with a husband and a coupla kids runnin' around the house."

"But Sally, you once told me you'd rather be in the theatre than do anything else in the whole world."

"Did I?" Sally laughed boisterously. "Maybe that's because I ain't never yet met Mr. Right."

Ella slumped in her seat. Will I ever know what I really want?

That same afternoon, the family, the Healys, and Bill witnessed Ella's performance for the first time. Afterward they all came trooping backstage.

"Gee Ella, it was swell!" Gertie was the first to proclaim. "We saw the show twice. Before the movie and after the movie."

Bill laughed. "And we enjoyed your performance both times."

Grace hugged her. "I feel so proud, Ella. It's thrilling to think that my best friend is a star on the stage!"

Charlie meanwhile was capering around like a young colt. "Ella you looked so funny dressed up like a little girl," he squealed.

"It was nice. Very nice," Papa added with a reassuring nod.

"Just nice, Papa? Why I thought it was marvelous!" Henny cried. She uttered a sigh of pure envy. "They all seemed to be having such a grand time. Boy, what a great

106

way to earn a living!" Suddenly inspired, she gripped Ella by the arm. "Say, why couldn't I be in an act like that? I can sing and dance as well as any one of those girls. Ella, you'll have to introduce me to the director!"

"Before you start making any plans for the future, first get through with high school," Mama said sharply. "Right now, one actress in the family is quite enough."

There was something in Mama's face that troubled Ella. I have the feeling she's not too happy with what I'm doing. Neither is Papa.

"You were so good, Ella," Sarah spoke up. "Only I wish they'd given you a real chance to show off your voice. You know. To sing something really nice."

"Well, maybe some day they will," Charlotte observed.

For the second week, the company moved on to another theatre in Brooklyn. Once again there were the slap-dash run-through, the backstage clutter, the heated arguments, the piling into a crowded dressing room—a dingy replica of the previous one—and finally the performance, despite all frustrations, running smoothly. Was it only a week ago that I was so bursting with excitement? Ella reflected through the mist of depression that clung to her. Only during those moments when she was actually performing did she feel her spirit lifting.

One morning, several days after the act moved to Yonkers, Ella came into the kitchen for her late breakfast. "Good morning, Mama," she said with forced heartiness.

"Good morning, Ella," Mama replied, pouring her some orange juice and measuring coffee into the percolator. "How's everything going?"

"Oh, the same. We move from one theatre to another,

but nothing really changes. There are other acts on the bill, but they don't seem much different. Last week the animal act was dogs and monkeys. This week it's a dancing bear. Last week, the song-and-dance team wore spats and straw hats and sporting canes. This week, it's baggy trousers with silly-looking caps. But the jokes they crack sound the same, and the soft-shoe routine is the same. Most of it is the same business over and over."

"It's not exactly the kind of thing that any of us had hoped for," Mama remarked.

Ella avoided Mama's glance. She touched her finger to the bowl of a spoon and traced its smooth shiny edge round and round. At length she looked up with some composure.

"I know, Mama"—she tried to frame the words carefully—"but we weren't any of us realistic. How else could I have gotten started? In opera? Not a chance! Maybe if I were to spend years with the finest teachers here, then go abroad for further study, it might possibly come to something. But that would cost a fortune! And where would we get that kind of money?"

She sipped at her orange juice. "And as for the concert stage," she went on, hoping her voice did not sound as dismal as she felt, "what manager would take a chance on a complete unknown with no experience? No. This is the only way for me. Actually I ought to consider myself lucky. There are loads of young people around singing their hearts out, and never getting a chance like this," she finished bleakly.

Mama's eyes were on her. Those candid, penetrating eyes. Surely they could see the conflict churning within her. As if from nowhere a whisper came—should I give it all up? The very thought was appalling. I can't! I've got a dream by the tail and I just can't let go. All the time I've spent! All the years! The money it's cost. It's unthinkable.

She stared down at the plate set before her. Mama had prepared the eggs exactly the way she liked them best. There were fresh crusty rolls too, spread with sweet butter. . . . Funny how your throat constricts when you're upset. She forced a mouthful down, then pushed the plate away.

"Aren't you feeling well?" Mama asked, a worried pucker forming between her eyes.

"Oh no! I'm fine!" Ella made a great effort at lightness. "Just not hungry."

"It seems to me you're never hungry lately," Mama said. She sat down at the table across from Ella, the knuckles of her hand pressed against her cheek. "Ella, I don't like the way you look. You're getting thin. And those dark circles under your eyes. What's wrong?"

"Nothing, Mama!" Ella flung out. "Please, stop fussing over me! I'm just too excited to eat—or sleep—that's all! It's all been so new and everything. I'll get used to it."

Will I? Will I ever? Abruptly she pushed her chair back. "I'm sorry, Ma, but I have to go. I'll be late."

13

Good-bye to All That

It was the evening of a final performance in Hoboken. In the dressing room, Ella tried vainly to concentrate on a book amid the banter shuffling back and forth around her.

"Listen, Irene, the feller I'm goin' out with tonight, he's got a friend. A real nice guy and he likes redheads especially. So how's about it?"

That's La Verne talking, Ella's ears registered, then couldn't help listening for Irene's answer.

"But I ain't dressed up for a date."

"Aw, go on! Hey, Sally, could you lend Irene that snazzy hat you bought? We're going out on a double."

"Sure. Irene, you want my green beads, too? They'd go real nice with your red hair."

Now Ella's attention was caught by a burst of staccato giggles from Dolly. "So, he says, 'Never mind about the sugar, baby. Just stir your finger in my cup.' "

"I ever tell you about the time the manager skipped out with the whole week's take?" Sally's voice floated again into Ella's consciousness. . . . "All our dough gone!"

"So what'd you do?"

"What do you think? The hotel had our suitcases. Wouldn't give 'em up till they got paid. I had to wire home for more dough."

"There ought to be a law."

The words blurred on the page of Ella's book. Suppose she had to wire home for funds. . . .

And now Jack was bending over her, his head so close, she twisted away. "Miss Highbrow, with her cutesy nose always in a book. Whatcha reading now, kid?"

He flipped the book over in her hand—*"My Antonia* by Willa Cather. . . . Not my *aunt*! Get it? Ha, hah! What's it all about?"

"Oh, about people in Nebraska. Homesteaders. Their hardships and . . ."

"How do you like that?" Jack cried, holding the book up for all to see. "As if we ain't got enough hardships of our own without havin' to read about some yokels in Nebraska." He tossed the book back in Ella's lap and wandered over to where several of the girls were playing cards on an up-ended suitcase.

Ella set the book aside. Suddenly it seemed so stuffy in the room. "Sally," she cried in exasperation, "I just can't get used to this waiting around between shows!"

Sally yawned comfortably. "It don't seem to bother me. I'm just lazy, I guess. That Jack! Don't pay any attention to him. Go on back to your reading."

"In all this commotion? I can't keep my mind on it." She indicated the players. "And I don't know how to play cards."

"Well, maybe you oughta learn," Sally advised. "It's a swell way of passin' the time. Especially on long train rides." Her mouth stretched wide in another yawn.

Passing time—passing time—the phrase kept revolving. That's exactly what I'm doing. And that's what I will be doing for months at a time. No chance to go on with

111

music lessons—no place for practice by myself—no time or energy for anything. She looked around the room, engulfed by the realization of how it would be. "I've got to get out of here!" she burst out. "I'm going down for a breath of air."

"You've only got fifteen minutes," Sally shouted after her.

Down the stairs, out the stage door, into the alley she fled, and then miraculously, she was in Jules's arms!

"Jules!" she exclaimed, half laughing, half crying. "What in the world are you doing here?"

"We have so little time left to be together, I had to see you."

They stood there wordless for several minutes. Ella could feel his quiet strength flow through her, all her vexation melting away.

"I've got to get back," she murmured. She pulled away reluctantly. "I'll meet you here right after the show."

As the company was lining up in the wings, Sally looked at her intently. "Say, you look like somebody just handed you a million bucks."

Ella smiled happily. "Jules was in the alley! Imagine!"

Sally regarded Ella's shining face. "You know," she observed dryly, "he's not gonna be waitin' for you outside every stage door. It's none of my business, but you can't have your cake and eat it too. You'd better make up your mind, kid, one way or the other. . . ."

Slowly, unwillingly, plowing her way through clouds of sleep, Ella awoke. She lay still, breathing in deeply the peace and quiet of the house. . . . Charlie and the girls must all be in school. And Mama, as usual, busy in the kitchen. These past weeks, how many things about the family have I missed? . . .

I'm grateful for these two weeks off before we go on tour. I must devote every minute to the family—to Jules. . . . When I think of leaving, I feel my insides all runny like an egg. She reached for her robe. I think I'll get up and lend a hand right now.

The kitchen air was filled with the delicious smell of baking which ordinarily marked Mama's preparations for the Sabbath. Against the bright sunlight streaming through the open window, Ella could see the waves of heat corkscrewing up from the stove.

"Good morning, Mama. It's so hot! In your condition, why are you baking? It's not Friday."

Mama looked up, smiling. "I'm almost finished. It didn't take too long. After all, it'll be quite a while before you'll be tasting your Mama's pies and filled cake." She wiped her forehead and went back to her work.

She's doing this for me. She knows I'm simply crazy about filled cake. It's utterly silly but I could just break down and weep over the mere thought of filled cake. She turned away quickly and went to the window.

A little sparrow was balancing its toothpick feet on a swaying clothesline. "Trr-reet!" Its tiny throat swelled with the effort. Somehow she was reminded of Professor Calvano. Strange. I haven't given a thought to my singing teacher all this time. He's like someone from another world. I must get to see him before I leave. . . . She turned back. Mama was already getting her breakfast for her. "Never mind, Mama," she cried. "Let me. I'll do it."

While Ella sipped her coffee, Mama's nimble fingers fluted the edges of dough around the rim of a pie plate.

Mama's always so capable, so strong, she thought . . . still . . .

Aloud she said, "Mama I feel so awful that I won't be here when the baby comes."

"It'll be all right, Ella," Mama assured her. "There's nothing for you to worry about. Tanta's coming to look after the house as always. She'll take perfect care of Papa and the children while I am in the hospital. She's even offered to stay on for a couple of weeks when I come home." She smiled a bit wanly. "It's funny but I must admit I feel a little strange about a hospital. All my other babies were born right at home with just the doctor and a midwife tending me."

Ella carried her breakfast dishes to the sink. Her hands fell agreeably into the rhythm of washing and drying. Washing dishes, she mused, putting them away in their accustomed places one by one—there's a kind of contentment in such homely tasks. Pleasure even, in seeing everything emerge clean and sparkling. Why should anyone think that homemaking hasn't creative aspects about it also? Like that pie, for instance. Only a real artist could turn out such creations. And the way we all enjoy them, I'm sure it must give Mama a tremendous sense of satisfaction.

"Ella, are you happy?"

Mama's unexpected question startled Ella out of her thoughts. Do mothers have a sixth sense about their children? she wondered. She fumbled about for a reply.

"Well," she responded finally, trying to measure every word, "I do enjoy performing. I enjoy it a lot. Naturally, I'm upset about going. Not really panicky, you understand," she amended quickly, "just a bit scared."

114

It isn't exactly the answer Mama may have hoped for, I know, but at least I'm trying to be honest—up to a point anyway.

Mama's breath was a faint sigh. "Is there anything I can do for you?" she inquired. "Some washing or ironing?"

"No, Mama. I can take care of those things myself. Well," she added with a show of briskness, "I'll go make up my bed."

Back in her room, Ella smoothed the sheets, plumped up the pillows, and flipped the bedspread. In the morning breeze the crisp white window curtains kept billowing out, then pressing back against the glass. The sun slanted across the bed as little dust particles danced up and down its golden band of light.

She sat down on the edge of the bed and let her eyes linger over each familiar detail—the dark mahogany desk polished satin-smooth—the comfortable armchair in which she curled up so often with a book—the small rug, its reds and greens and deep blues sharply outlined against the parquet floor—the bedstead with its gleaming brass rods and knobs. A little stab of pain pinched her heart. She was going to miss this tiny room so long shared with Sarah.

The umpah-pah of a small German band floated up from below. She hummed along with the folksy melody for a while, then took a nickel from her purse, wrapped it in a bit of paper, and tossed it down.

A moment of silence and the band was playing the old favorite—"O Fir Tree Tall.". . . She was a little girl again and it was Mama who was singing the tune to her. . . .

Suddenly she felt as if she were stifled. She had to get

out. Hurriedly she dressed and dashed down the stairs into the street.

As she walked along, she found herself looking at everything with eyes that seemed brand-new. The little old woman watering her flower pots on her stoop—a horse clip-clopping by, patiently pulling a cart laden with fresh fruit and vegetables—the butcher on the corner in straw hat and white apron, hanging a rope of sausages in his window . . .

She strolled on. Up ahead was the squat red brick schoolhouse which Charlotte and Gertie attended. It must be recess time, for the schoolyard was alive with little girls. Some were playing tag or bouncing balls. Others stood around or chased one another. A small group just in front of Ella was chanting to the slip-slap of a rope.

> *On the mountain stands a lady.*
> *All she wants is a nice young man. . . .*

All I want is a nice young man. Ella squeezed her eyes shut. Are you sure that's all you want? A solitary tear made its way down her cheek.

Ella's finger reached for the door buzzer. She hesitated. Why had she come? she wondered. All she could feel was that she had a compelling need to talk to Professor Calvano. When finally she pressed the button, she could hear him calling out, "Come in, come in, Ella! The door she is open."

As she entered, the professor was busily scooping up assorted music sheets from his sofa. He greeted her warmly, all the while looking around his cluttered studio for a place to put the accumulated pile. It ended up being dumped on the piano.

Bounding back to the sofa, he patted the faded cushion beside him and said, "Sit now, Ella, and we talk. You look a little more thin than before. Tell me, are you excited about starting on your tour?"

Ella shook her head. "No, Professor."

He eyed her keenly. "You're sad maybe about leaving your Jules?"

"Yes. But it's more than that. I keep wondering whether what I am leaving him for is worth the sacrifice."

"I think I understand. I didn't tell you but I went to see the show. You were very good. But"—his shoulders lifted— "after all, there's music and there's music. Is it not so?"

Ella's head lowered. The professor took her hands in his. "My poor little Ella," he murmured. "What is it you want to make of your life?"

When at last she could look up, her face appeared almost stricken. It seemed an effort for her to speak.

"I want so desperately to sing, Professor. But I feel trapped in a world that somehow is not for me. It's gotten to the point where I have come to hate what I'm doing."

The professor nodded. "Yes, I see." He rose and strode to the piano. Ruffling his fingers over the keys, he began to play the opening bars of "Knowest Thou That Fair Land."

"Your favorite," he said, giving her a broad smile. He continued to play softly. "Ella, there is a way out for you. I did not want to say something before, because you and your mother were so excited by the big chance. There is a place in my choral group. Look, this spring our final concert is in Town Hall and we do Mendelssohn's *Elijah*.

117

"Few of us will ever be famous. I can tell you none of us will be rich. But we will have more important riches—the joy of making the beautiful music."

The playing ended. "You think about it, Ella."

As Ella and Jules entered the park, her hand in his, Ella could feel the disquieting thoughts of the day receding. She felt suddenly lighter than a bubble, freer than air. She could hardly contain the happy little laugh that kept springing from her throat.

They sauntered past the entrance gate into the broad expanse of inviting green. Already the setting sun had enkindled a scarf of blazing colors—violet, crimson, and gold—along the horizon. From behind the darkening trees there came the faint hum of traffic. In the distance they could see the twinkling chain of lights which was the elevated station. The moment was magical; the world was remote.

They sat down on a bench near the small pond. The air was damply cool. Around them was stillness, and now the impatient moon, wheeling across the opposing sky, trailed silver on the placid water. Jules held her close.

All at once a voice inside her enunciated loud and clear—vaudeville is not for me. She drew a deep breath, her gaze losing itself in a scattering of leaves whirling by.

"A penny for your thoughts, Ella."

"Jules," she responded quietly, "I've made up my mind. I'm leaving the show."

"Leaving the show?" he repeated.

She nodded. "I know now it's not the kind of career I really want."

Jules stared at her. "Ella, are you sure you know what you're saying?"

"Yes." She groped for the right words. "Somehow—it doesn't seem important to me—any longer. Don't think I've decided this on the spur of the moment. I've been thinking and thinking about it night and day. I just wasn't sure up to now."

"Then how can you be sure now?"

She considered for a long moment before answering. "I went to see Professor Calvano today. He helped me clear up my own misgivings. He opened up my eyes to what I was unwilling to admit to myself. I realize now that I couldn't be completely dedicated to that sort of life. I'd be willing to make all kinds of sacrifices if I thought it was worth it. But it just isn't—for me, that is. There's nothing wrong with the vaudeville act. It would be a lucky break for another kind of person. It was just me that was all wrong."

Jules cupped her face in his hands. "Ella, to have you stay here makes me very happy. But I wouldn't want you to give up your singing."

"I won't have to. Professor Calvano has asked me to join his choral group."

"Will that be enough for you?"

"Oh yes, yes! I'll be able to go on studying and singing the kind of music that is dear to me. Also it means I'll be staying home with the family. Best of all, I shall be near you. Oh Jules, how marvelous it's going to be for both of us. Both of us studying and working. And who knows, perhaps some day another kind of career opportunity may come along."

For a while nothing more was said. Then Jules spoke. "How are your parents going to take this?"

Ella shook her head. "I don't know. It's Mama I'm

119

mostly worried about. She had this dream of a great career for her daughter. To make up for her own lost chance, I suppose. But actually I don't think she was too happy about vaudeville." She sighed. "All those months wasted—"

"Nothing one has learned is ever a waste," Jules assured her.

"I guess so," Ella agreed. "And not earning a living at it will not make me love music any the less. My studying has given me a better understanding and a greater joy in music than I ever would have had. And besides, I can still sing for people. There are plenty of places where good amateurs are needed." She smiled up at Jules. "We'll be able to sing together in Temple. Won't that be wonderful? And some day I'll be able to sing to my children."

"Our children, Ella."

Her head burrowed in his shoulder, her finger tracing a circle on the button of his jacket.

"I love you, Ella," Jules said softly as he kissed her.